DARKNESS WITHIN

By Kev Carter

Copywrite

ISBN:

978-1-326-97998-0

2017

Please visit my website

www.fancyacoffee.wix.com/kev-carter-books

Other titles by this author

Twisted Blood
Tales of Horror and Torment
Tales of Horror and Torment 2
Hidden Darkness
Sisters of Darkness
Realms of Darkness
Back into Darkness
Shadows of Darkness
Dreams of Darkness
Beyond the Darkness
Depths of Darkness
Darkness of Ray Sibson
Darkness
Darkness within

CHAPTER ONE

Sunnycliffe Woods is a quiet place, beautiful in autumn, bleak in winter and idyllic in Summer, Spring time brought the fresh, new life to its heart and soul.

But this wood has a secret, a secret that was deep under its large tree roots, the secret kept for many, many years and never discovered, a dark and horrid secret that no one knew about except those involved, anyone who did know, has long gone, rather died with it or met an untimely death looking for it. Many people walk right past it, right over it and never know, Animals have come to accept its existence and tend to just go about their daily lives and ignore it, but sometimes, there is an unfortunate soul who comes across it or is driven unknowingly towards it, like a silent invisible pack running its prey to the waiting comrades in hiding who pounce and kill the running scared victim. It is then dragged off and never to be seen again, some poor tramp or down and out might rest their weary head down for the night only never to see the morning, never missed.

Their underground dwellers have been around for as long as the dark arts themselves, servants or the darkness at one time held high up with respect, but long forgotten and now just left to fend for themselves, they never moved up and on, the way the other minions of darkness did, they refused to die out and went underground, literally. They live under forests and woods searching out food and hunting down their prey with stealth and silence, they venture in catacombs of tunnels and warrens they have dug out over the years, spanning across large areas and under graveyards so they can use the fresh buried for their cannibalistic tastes. No one knows how many are left or where they all are, but they still exist. Still there waiting and still would serve any darkness that came along and commanded it. They have become a forgotten community of evil beings that are despicable and vile. They have devised a chamber where they live and tunnels up to the surface with ingenious flaps like trap doors that are perfectly hidden to any passerby. Springing them open and grabbing any unsuspecting victim, dragging them down and silently gone from the world for ever. It is done within seconds and the flap securely shut afterwards leaving no sign or sound. It is something they have honed to a fine art over the years. Living in darkness they have increased sense of smell and hearing which is how they hunt and survive. Living a life of outcast forgotten creatures they dwell underground and hunt and eat anything they can find, nothing is wasted and nothing is excluded from their diet. Underground springs supply their water they have learned and adapted to the life they have they do very well indeed.

Walking along the path unaware of the grotesque creatures that live below were people going about their evening, enjoying the wonders and peacefulness of the trees and forest around them, it is a wonderful place if you can relate and feel its beauty, different people see it in different ways, some find sanctuary and solitude some find excitement and adventure. But whatever people see, they never see the hidden truth below or if they do it is too late for them.

Helen was a domineering woman and always had to be right, she was nowhere near as clever as she thought she was but would never admit it. Her husband went along with her just for a quiet life. They were walking with backpacks on and a large tent compacted down into a four foot long holdall it was very heavy, but she expected him to carry it like the donkey she used him as, she would pick the spot, she would tell him where to pitch the tent, and she would sit and watch and criticise him while he did. They had been walking for some time and he was out of breath and his arm was aching from carrying the heavy holdall but he didn't complain, it would just bring on a barrage of criticism and insults from her. She stopped and looked round the green and brown leaves scattered on the ground the trees reaching up high and standing proud and strong. Majestic and powerful. Helen looked back at her husband who was welcoming the break in pace, she rolled her eyes and searched again around the area, she liked the look of it and decided this would make a nice place to rest down for the night, she loved camping but didn't like the hard work involved, which is where he came in. She nodded and turned to her husband saying.

"Here is good I like it here, pitch the tent here will you" she went and sat on a nearby rock and stretched her legs out she ran her hands through her hair and didn't lift a finger to help him put up the tent, he didn't really mind because everything had to be done her way even if it was wrong so it suited him to be left alone. She eased the light back pack off her back and placed it in front of her she opened the top and took out a small bottle of water unscrewing the top she took a mouthful and watched the tent gradually being put together. She leaned back and enjoyed the sounds and sights of her surroundings closing her eyes she took a deep breath of the gorgeous clear unpolluted air around her.

He was making good progress, he had done this many times and at least now he was not shouted at or criticised as he worked. He methodically erected the steel tubing, then the ground sheet then the tent itself. He made sure it was sturdy and everything was where it should be. It didn't take him long and he was glad when he was done he sat down and wiped the sweat from his brow and took along deep breath. He searched in his packed and heavy backpack for some water and took a much needed drink himself. She noticed the tent was up and ready, she did her obligatory check round it to make sure it was done correctly and to her liking. He just started to unpack and arrange everything sooner he got it done sooner he could have a well earned and needed rest.

The night crept in and they had settled for the evening, it was a warm night and clear they had sat out looking up at the stars for a while before coming into the tent and settling down. She was content and in a warm sleeping bag she had paid a lot of money for. He was in a cheaper one but it did the same job, she loved the camping and sleeping out he hated it but did it for a quiet life. The nights calm was here, soon the sounds of the nocturnal animals would be heard if you listened right. But the sounds round this tent were very different and very slight. They had been watched for a while now and hidden eyes spied them intensely. Noses smelling the air for scent and odour crouched and laid in waiting ready. Silently moving into position and checking every direction and angle they circled and had settled now, it was a system they had perfected and worked as a pack to ensure once they attacked it was done quickly and they were gone without trace as soon as possible.

"Don't you just love the outdoors and the thrill of it all" she said looking happy all curled up in her sleeping bag.

"Yes it is really satisfying" he said curled up in his, his face not agreeing with what his mouth just said to her.

"Yes it is, one with nature and out in the wilds you can't beat it, keep all your sunny beaches and expensive hotels, they have nothing on this" she really believed what she was saying and smiled to herself as she snuggled into her expensive sleeping bag.

He closed his eyes slowly and just wanted to tell her the truth but he never did, he just swallowed his thoughts and stayed quiet. She mumbled away at how wonderful it all was and he just grunted an agreement here and there, he had heard it all before. Then he lifted his head, a sound, a noise, he heard it twice. He turned his head and listened again. The light in the tent was an old style looking lamp but it was powered by batteries. He could not see anything outside but he was sure he had heard something. Her voice became second to his hearing, it was late and the night was well developed. It was not a sound he had heard before it was not like an animal passing or rummaging it was more of a movement then a stop then a movement again. He sat up and strained his ears. There was more than one, the noise was all over and from different directions. He got to his knees and looked towards the flap in the tent.

"What are you doing?" His wife asked turning to look at him.

"There is something moving outside" he said without looking at her.

"Well yes there will be, it is forest you daft idiot, settle down and go to sleep" she turned her head and ignored him settling back into her sleeping bag.

"I am just going to check don't want it to be bloody kids messing about"

He searched for the little torch in his bag then quietly and slowly he opened the flap of the tent and went out. He shone the light around but could see nothing unusual he crawled out on all fours then stood up he searched the area as far as the little torches beam would allow he strained his eyes and peered round the area, walking further away from the tent as he did.

It was some while before she realised he had not returned she looked up and round the tent. Annoyed and shaking her head she sighed out. She listened and heard the thud outside the flap and then there was silence, she looked and listened.

"What are you doing, come back in" she shouted

There was no reply and she listened trying to hear a sound, she could call out to but there was nothing.

An uneasy feeling that crept over her, she suddenly felt alone and scared, she shouted out his name again but still there was no answer. The silence bore down on her, the darkness outside seemed heavy and full of danger all of a sudden.

She screamed once has she saw the flap open violently and two creatures dart in, she didn't scream again and she was dead before she could draw breath. Her throat cut with well practiced skill and accuracy. Her body dragged away and the area cleared in a matter of minutes, working as a team they carried the two bodies away and the remaining ones cleared the area taking everything and leaving no trace. One last one scattered dirt over the blood stains outside the tent then they were gone, off away into the trees and quietly disappeared. Silence once again and no sign of anything unusual. The night carried on and the day would break as if nothing had happened.

Yet another disappearance and yet another mystery of these woods, taken underground and disposed of in some way, no trace and no clues. It was not the first and it would not be the last, evil existed here and it was well hidden but always watching, always listening and every now and then it showed and struck with savagery and brutality then was gone again. People were not safe here but it was made all the more dangerous that they didn't know it until it was much too late.

CHAPTER TWO

The rain pelted down but Ray didn't notice he was stood solid and rooted to the spot looking at the grave stone, Bodie was by his side, he felt uneasy, there was strangeness in the air something didn't feel right but he had no idea what it was.

Darius was stood behind Ray and eventually spoke to him after staying silent since bringing him to the grave side.

"I texted you Ray and rang but there was no answer on your phone, did you not feel anything at all, did you not know?" Darius asked with a confused frown on his face.

"No, no nothing I do not know why but I had no idea, how long was she ill?"

"After we last saw you she seemed to be back to her old self she had come to terms with it and was going back to her life and work, she seemed fine, then suddenly she took ill and it was so rapid she went downhill so quickly" he shook his head and bowed it with sadness.

"What happened, what was it she had?" Ray still was not looking away from the grave stone or moving even though the rain pelted his face.

"The official report said pneumonia, but I do not believe they actually knew to be honest"

"She died quickly, not in pain, no suffering?"

"Not much really, no, it was very sudden I was with her when she passed away, she was in my arms and spoke your name, and it was the last word she said"

Ray closed his eyes and sighed, he looked down at Bodie and then round the area he could feel something, something present but not seen, he had felt it before but this time it was very strong. Bodie moved and sniffed at the earth on the grave in front of him, then looked at Ray who looked down at him and nodded.

Darius didn't really understand, but he didn't interfere, he was feeling uncomfortable standing in the pouring rain but he had to bring Ray here, he had to show him the grave where Christine was buried, she was put in the earth over a month ago. Ray had come back to get his car legal which Darius did every year for him with Insurance, MOT and service. It was then that he had told him the news about Christine, Ray wanted taking to the grave side straight away. He had stood here for a long time and the rain had not stopped in that time. Finally he turned and looked at Darius his face dripping wet like the rest of him.

"She didn't die of pneumonia, she is not at rest there is something wrong here, the whole place doesn't feel right, Bodie senses it too"

"What are you going to do?" Darius asked wiping the rain from his eyes.

"Go get out of these clothes and shower then we will talk more about what happened I want every detail leave nothing out no matter how small" he walked past Darius and down to this car with Bodie following, Darius looked at Christine's grave once again then the sadness filled him so he turned and went to join Ray in his car.

The rain pelted the grave stone the soil soaking it up as it bounced off the granite and hit the soil, it was empty now no one here but Ray had felt something just like his dog did he was not sure what it was but he didn't like it, he could not understand why he had not felt anything when she died, but then why should he?

Driving back Ray didn't say much and Darius didn't push any conversation, it was not a long drive and they were soon at the house. Darius went in and made some phone calls to service Ray's car and sort out everything else like he always did every year. Ray went for a shower and took Bodie with him, who he gave a bath afterwards, it was always a struggle to bathe Bodie he was a large dog and loved the warm water and soap in his fur he dashed around like a big puppy when he was finally lifted out of the bath and was ready to dry. Ray wrapped him in a large towel and rubbed him all over, but he play fought and dashed about so in the end Ray just let him do his mad twenty minutes like dogs do.

They settled down all washed and cleaned up, Ray shaved and got fresh clothes on he used the washing machine to clean the ones he had taken off, it was normally a time to recharge and clean up and re pack, build up on supplies and generally relax for a few days but this time was different. There was sadness in the air, the death of Christine had affected a lot of people, friends had come to the funeral and all had noticed Ray was not there, some understood, some were confused but no one said anything bad about it.

"Your car goes in day after tomorrow, full service and MOT, make you legal again "Darius told Ray has he come from the other room.

"Cheers, it needs some pads on the front and the tyres are getting low on tread too"

"I have told him to make it like new" Darius smiled as he said this line every year at this time, he sat across from Ray on a sofa, in the large front room, the open fire was glowing steady and giving the room and soft cosy feel. Bodie had settled down and was laid out on his side enjoying of the warmth of the fire. Ray in the large leather chair just off to the left was doing the same; he was facing Darius who looked at him and could see he was working on something in his head.

"Did she say anything was wrong before she died?" Ray said, not looking at Darius but into the fire and watched the small flames dancing their dance.

"She said she felt ill and funny, but she had been down for a long time she perked up and seemed to be doing really well just before ..." he bowed his head and felt sad as he spoke of it, and remembered her dying in his arms.

"Did you feel anything strange around the house, anything happen out of the ordinary?"

"I was worried for her and to be honest I didn't, the doctor came and said he wanted to do some tests but it all happened so quickly, she seemed to spiral downhill and refused to go into hospital she died shortly after" Darius was confused and sad, he watched Ray and wondered how he could hold in and show no emotion he thought the one person he would shoe emotion over would be her but there seemed to be nothing.

"They did an autopsy and said it was pneumonia, then the funeral took place and here we are ,have you not noticed the darkness here Darius, maybe it covered its self well with everyone but I can sense it, there is a presence a strong one but it is hiding its self in a way, hard to detect but it is there, watching"

"I have felt nothing, nothing has happened out of the ordinary"

"Except a healthy woman took ill and died in your arms you mean?" Ray said not looking at him, but was deep in thought.

"Of course that Ray, I mean nothing supernatural nothing was reported and no one felt anything or witnessed anything"

"Like I said its well hidden but it is there, cloaked and waiting it must of got to her somehow and did it very cleverly, it took her and is now still here probably waiting for me, it must of tricked her or maybe it was something she was not scared of but whatever it was it got her"

"What could it be, why did she not know it was evil why would she not say anything?" Darius didn't know what to think, he respected Ray but he was not sure if this was right or wrong.

"Maybe it came to her as something else, maybe it was disguised, I don't know did she not say anything at all to you, anything?"

"Her last word was your name that is all, she couldn't really speak; you don't think it came disguised as you?" Darius raised his voice on the last two words of his sentence has he realised what Ray was saying and how he could of missed something right before his eyes.

"Possibly, but she was very acute, would she be fooled like that, what state of mind was she in was she strong was she vulnerable?"

"Like I said she seemed to perk up a lot, get back on her feet and on with her life, but then this happened out for the blue, he stopped and thought about what he was saying Ray let him then carry on with his train of thought, you are not saying she thought you had come back she got tricked into thinking you were in touch with her, that is why she was happy then something go to her disguised as you?" he had a very worried look on his face and his mind was searching for clues that he might of missed at the time now he had this new evidence.

"Was she having nightmares, or did she say she felt any presence, was she using her cards?"

"I don't think so, she never said if she had nightmares at the end, I know she use to have some before, but she never seemed bothered about them, the cards I don't think she was using them as much or at all to be honest, she was trying to readjust and get her life back, does it weaken you Ray, now that she is gone?"

"No, it doesn't but I feel something is wrong, something is not right here I think something got to her or took her, she is not at peace"

"Is it just a feeling, or have they done it to get to you or is there something else you are not telling me?"

"Just a feeling, I have no idea what it is but I have no doubt I will find out" he looked up from the fire at Darius and stared him in the eye, coldly without emotion.

It turned Darius cold and sent a shiver through his body, he was still hurting at losing Christine but Ray seemed to of shut off, but then again he rarely showed any feelings.

"We will talk more tomorrow my friend I am now going to bed and will leave you in peace as always you know to treat the place as your own" Darius gave him a smile and quietly left the room and went up to bed.

Ray returned his gaze to the fire, the flames still dancing up and reaching above the glow of the wood that sat below them. His thoughts cast back to the first time he saw Christine, a small figure walking up the hillside to meet him a woman who had tracked him down and came to be by his side, he thought of the fights they been in the battles they had fought, he remembered the arguments when they lived together how he struggled to be domestic and could not do it, he remembered the times he had saved her life and all the times she had been there for him. He took a deep breath and closed his eyes he rubbed his face with both hands and yawned he stood up and went up stairs to bed, Bodie followed and they both fell into a restless sleep.

The next day it was bright and the sun was out, pushing the rain clouds away and brightening the whole world up to a warmer and sunnier place, or so it seemed anyway. Ray was up early, taking everything from the boot of his car, he emptied it and laid his tent out to air dry in the heat of the sun, he used this time to restock and to repair any damage he had, be it to the car or his equipment. He worked in silence and was alone with his thoughts. Bodie was laid out a few yards from him, his head on his paws watching. Darius knew when to leave Ray alone and this was one of them times.

 Methodically he checked everything, discarding anything that was no good or broken making a mental note of what he needed to replace or anything new he might need. The car was left empty to go to Darius's friend who had the garage and it would be serviced checked and any work that needed doing would be done. Then Ray would restock it once again with all his weapons and equipment and supplies. Normally he would then be away, but this time there was something he had to sort out. The darkness he could feel, but it was a strange one, something he had not encountered before. He would confront his Ouija later but for now he had this job to do and carried on with it. Watched by Bodie and looked at now and again by Darius but left alone which is what he wanted.

The car was ready and waiting to be taken for the next day, all Ray's items were safe in the house there was nothing to do now but wait. The chill time was welcomed and the warmth of the house and good hot food was also welcomed, both Ray and Bodie enjoyed it while they could. it was something he liked only now and again he seemed not to be able to settle for a long period of time in a house maybe it was because he shared one from time to time, he liked his own company and was more at ease with himself than anyone else, so living with someone was always a struggle and he never settled or did it very well. But that was not a problem anymore he never saw himself living with anyone again. He sat in a garden chair looking out across the well trimmed and cared for lawn at the back of Darius's house. Bodie was laid out on his side on the cool grass his eyes were open but he was totally relaxed and calm. Darius brought a large mug of tea out, seeing he had just made himself one, he gave it to Ray and handed him a full packet of unopened milk chocolate biscuits, Ray nodded in appreciation and gladly took them he sipped his tea and dunked his biscuits has he looked out across the lawn seemingly deep in thought but looking relaxed.

He had a visitor mid afternoon it was Jan, the doctor who had helped him and Christine once, she was always asking about him to Darius and she was a white witch of high standing she took this chance and opportunity to come and see Ray, he didn't mind, she had been a very good ally at one point and he never forgot things like that. A large woman as he remembered, but she had lost some weight and looked fit and healthy she wore a light top and casual trousers. She was an attractive woman and more so because of her intelligence Ray thought. He chatted with her and told her some of the things that had happened she listened with interest and concern, she had always had a thing for him and always would, she had never known anyone like the warrior has he was known in her circles. She had concerns about Christine, although she had not seen her herself, she knew the doctor who did and he sent her to the hospital. Ray was none the wiser about it he knew there was something very wrong but had no idea what, Jan was a wonderful woman and he enjoyed her company for an hour or so before she left. Hugging him a little longer then she needed and giving him a kiss on the lips she smiled and told him.

"If I can do anything, anything at all for you please do not hesitate to come and see me Ray" He smiled and nodded, knowing she meant every word, he stood up and stretched his large frame out groaning as he did. Walking back into the house he saw it was empty, Darius must of gone out. He went up stairs and then froze on the landing, the feeling hit him like an electric shock, there was a presence, he looked round carefully, his senses heightened, he didn't move just looked round, he could feel it. He heard the giggle of a woman, not a happy giggle or childish, but a malevolent one, the same giggle the insane give just after they have murdered someone or tortured something it was not a good sound. He slowly walked across the landing and listened again, not too sure which room the sound had come from. He walked silently listening intensely, then he heard the malicious laugh again. it was the same voice as before and it was coming from the room that was his while he was here. He walked to the half open door and pushed it in so he could see what was inside.

She looked at him half grinning half snarling her face contorted and her head tilted to one side. Her eyes wide but sunken into her skull her skin was a pale yellow, she blinked and her eye balls turned jet black. Dressed in a strange leather costume like from centuries ago, the same thing Angelique would have worn; she stared at him and laughed a devilish laugh. It was Christine, she was stood here in front of him she was possessed and he was only feet away from her. He stood his ground and gritted his teeth together, she was going to play on his emotions, he knew he could not show any or they would have a foot hold, a kink in his armour. Something he could not afford, she spoke and the voice was deep and rough not of a woman but of something evil and powerful.

"We have her, she is with us now, and you soon will be, your time has finally come, you are only a few steps from hell"

Before Ray answered he heard the thumping sound of Bodie racing up the stairs and passed him charging into the room, his teeth snarling and the fur up on his back he stood between Ray and this thing that looked like Christine. It stared down at him and bared its teeth back but didn't move did not show any sign of power or magic. It looked up at Ray again and in Christine's voice said.

"We will be together again my love and this time it will be in darkness, it is much easier and much more fun" she smiled and laughed out her voice changing back to the coarse violent one as before. Bodie was waiting for the command he stood his ground guarding his master Ray said nothing and looked this thing straight into its black evil eyes. It looked back at him in the same way. It was a stand off until Ray spoke He seemed calm and relaxed as he smiled and said

"Whoever you are, this is your mistake, if you think this is going to work for one moment you are sadly and stupidly mistaken, you have no chance in fucking hell of getting to me this way" he shook his head and let out a unconcerned laugh.

"It is you who is mistaken, let the fun commence then" it snarled and dashed forward but was gone, disappeared like an entity before it got to him or Bodie. The room was silent and Ray felt nothing there now, Bodie went to where it had been standing and sniffed the floor, he felt nothing either. Whatever it was now gone, Ray took a deep breath and looked round the room, at least now he knew what to expect, he had not shown any emotion or concern at seeing Christine which was imperative, that is what he did. It was testing him and no doubt would test him again. The rest of the day passed uneventfully and the darkness of the night dropped in without problem, he told Darius and they discussed it, but Darius knew he must leave this to Ray, but as Ray said if she shows herself to him, he must not be fooled or tricked into anything, he understood and tried to accept it, Darius did not sleep that night, Bodie did not either keeping guard over Ray who rested and was only disturbed once from the giggling outside in the garden where Christine was stood for a short time looking up at him from the lawn. But she was not there for long it was just a test and done for effect, Ray was not stupid and was very well experienced, he knew the game they were playing but was not sure if this was Christine or not yet, it might be her or it might be a trick. he would find out in time no doubt but for now he had to stay focused and strong.

The next day he took his car into the garage himself he wanted to get out of the house for a little while and go for a walk into town as well, he left Bodie sleeping and drove to the garage the man there knew all about him and was waiting for him. Pulling up to the large shed that looked like it would fall down at anytime he stopped and got out of the car, the place was a typical good mechanics place mucky and looked in disarray, but he had no doubt they knew where everything was when they wanted it. There was an inspection pit and various bits of motors and cars scattered all round, when you find a good mechanic like this you stuck with him he knew what he was doing and would not cheat you. Ray liked the place, he would not trust it if it was clean and too neat and tidy, they had too much time on their hands if it was so.

"Ray, good to see you" a voice said from the side of the shed followed by a small man but with a powerful build, he came up to him, Ray noticed he had a slight limp on his left side and looked well worn out and hard worked.

"Hello" was all Ray said but with a friendly tone they shook hands and they both admired the strong grip they gave.

"Full service MOT the front disks need doing and a couple of tires.." Ray was saying but was stopped in mid sentence.

"Mr Sibson it will all be done, the car will be done to a very high standard and only original and good quality parts will be fitted I will give it my best and fullest of attention"

"Then I am sure it will be perfect" Ray said with admiration he liked this man instantly a real working class and down to earth sort, they are a dying breed as Ray only too well knew.

"Thank you glad you feel so, I will work on it today I have nothing else booked and will spend all day on it if necessary"

"You are by yourself here, no help?"

"I tried to get the lad interested but he is not bothered, you won't have children I expect?"

"No, not what I know of, never really got on with them to be honest"

"Well you and me both my lad he is a disgrace they all seemed to be the bloody same, bone idle, selfish no bloody idea"

"I know, it is ridiculous the youth of today they are just soft as shite"

"He stays in his fucking room playing games all day, ask him to do anything he throws a tantrum, his mother doesn't help of course, treating him like a bloody child all the time spoiling him, giving in to him"

"Doesn't do them any good, you have got to discipline them a good clip round the lug hole never hurt anybody"

"Exactly that is just what I say, they have no idea of the real world, and they cannot handle crisis or any drama they run away from it or just throw a panic attack"

"No common sense either, we should throw them all in the army as soon as they leave school" Ray said liking this man more and more.

"I have said that, bring back national service, when you were sixteen you left school got a job, not well paid but you worked, you made your mistakes you learned about life had your fun, fuck sake now they reach sixteen stay on at collage then possibly university they don't fucking leave school until they are twenty"

"Put into a false sense of security, no fucking idea of the real world, like you say that few years is your growing time, making you into a man they don't have that now" Ray knew where this man was coming from and agreed with him totally.

"They have no backbone no respect, want everything without working for it, they want it now and if they don't get it they cry about it, ungrateful selfish soft cheeky little fuckers"

"I know where you are coming from with that, the world is going soft, society is fucked, looks after the guilty and pisses on the innocent, attitudes are all wrong"

"They don't want to get their hands dirty, want it easy every time, I tried to get him to work here, learn a trade set up a business, no chance, too much like hard work, I just don't understand them I can tell you"

"I take it you only have the one then?"

"Thank fuck, I suppose some are not that bad but when you live with one like I have, you tend to tar them all with the same brush" he shook his head and sighed out.

"Yeah I know what you mean, they need to get out when they are kids, climb trees get into fights, eat worms, they do fuck all now, just stay in and get fat and pale from watching TV all day and playing games"

"When I was a kid I was never in, out all the time"

"Me, too, came in when the street lights came on, your mum shouted you and you ignored it, then your dad said shouted your name once and you fucking came in straight away"

"That's it, yes that is just it, that is a real childhood out playing and exploring and interacting with people, I don't know bloody kids of today"

"It is only going to get worse, the working man is becoming a thing of the past, I was working with my dad on the roof tops when I was fourteen"

"Yep, I was working every weekend here with my dad, then went to school while still grafting here for him and he passed it all on to me when he died"

"It is a lost time and a dying generation" Ray said with a hint of regret in his voice.

They both nodded and Ray said his good bye he knew he had left his car in good hands and when he picked it up it would be done to the highest standard.

He walked into town and thought about Christine and the way she had visited him or if it had been her at all. He was not going to yield under that emotional pressure but wondered if Darius would in some way. he came to a cafe and went in he ordered a large coffee and got a piece of cake to go with it he sat by the window and waited for the uninterested girl to bring it to him, she put them both down on the table and without a smile or thank you, and went away again to the counter. He looked out at the town moving along as it must have done for many years, people just walking along not talking not looking at each other, most young people looking at their phones in their hands they didn't even seem to be looking where they were going. The old lady struggling with her one small bag of shopping no one paying her any attention, cars moving along not giving way always seeming to be rushing, it seemed to him the world is moving too fast and no one cares about it. He was lost in his thoughts for a while until a familiar face smiled at him from the pavement outside it was Jan. Ray smiled back and nodded knowing she would come in, and she did just that.

"Ray, how the hell are you, hope you don't mind me joining you, or do you?" she stopped and waited for the answer she would respect whatever it might be.

"No of course not, grab a coffee and sit down" Ray said with a genuine smile.

She gladly did and was facing him with her hands round the mug she had in front of her within minutes.

"You were deep in thought is everything alright?" she asked looking him in the eye her lips slightly apart

"Depends how you look at it I suppose, but I will sort it" Ray said noncommittal

"Well, you know to ask me for any help if you need it don't you?"

"Yes I do and thank you for that, Tell me Jan, when did you last see Christine alive?"

"It must have been several month before she became ill I think, why?"

"Did you notice anything wrong at all, I know we talked about it yesterday but there is something wrong and I am not sure what the hell it is going to cause"

"I felt nothing then but when at the Funeral there was a strange feeling a lot of friends were there, some asked about you but it was a quiet affair really, but like I said there was something there some strange.." she searched for a word with a frown on her face

"Presence, feeling you was being watched?" Ray asked taking a sup of his coffee.

"Yes, yes that is it, what is happening Ray something is wrong I can feel it"

"She came to visit me yesterday or something that looked and sounded like her did but I am not convinced it is her to be honest I would say she is still in the ground at the cemetery"

"Bloody hell Ray, she has come back ?" she was genuinely concerned and believed instantly, if anyone else had told her this she would be sceptical and her professionalism would take over but because it was Ray she believed every word he said to her.

"I don't know I don't think so, something is using her or just imitating her to get to us, I am just concerned it might work on certain people if it visits them"

"Like whom? Now you have told me I will be aware, not that I feel she would come to me anyway, all the sisters have made their concerns felt, we all want to help you Ray you know that you can call on us at any time don't you?" her words were full of truth.

"Yes, I know, thank you, but we will have to wait and see, looks like it wants to play silly games first" he sighed out and took another drink of his coffee and a bite of his cake.

"Are you getting tired Ray, you cannot go on forever, you might have to think of a time when you stop?"

"When I stop I am dead, they will always come for me no matter where I am or what I am doing, no, I cannot stop, it will be time to die when I do"

Jan looked at him she didn't show it but felt sadness for him, he had just said something that struck at her heart and she was saddened by it, knowing their warrior would inevitably die one day, he seems invincible and unstoppable but will his day come and when will it come? She smiled and took a drink to give herself a few moments to adjust to her feeling then she put her coffee cup down and carried on in the same tone of voice as before.

"So what are you going to do, can I do anything for you in any way?"

"Don't know depends on what happens, I will react to an action whatever that is at the time, but thank you for your help and thank your friends for me too, do you still have that bloody automatic you used some years ago?"

"I keep my hand in yes, illegal of course. but what the hell?" she said as if in passing.

"I was impressed with you at that time and nothing has changed Jan you are one hell of a woman "

"Do you need to borrow it, might come in handy?"

"No, thank you, but I do appreciate your concern" he finished his cake and looked like he didn't have a care in the world he was very good at not showing his emotions or his feelings, and Jan liked this but she didn't really understand why.

"How long you staying here do you know yet?"

"No idea yet I could leave and hope whatever it is follows but I am not sure it would so I might have to stay until it is destroyed"

"You amaze me do you know that? You just take it all in your stride don't you?"

"Not really but like I said I don't really have a choice anymore, if I stop I am dead" He looked up at her and then out of the window and back at her again she knew not to push the subject.

"Sorry, didn't mean to pry" she felt a little embarrassed and annoyed at herself for pushing the subject seeing Ray had a lot on his mind, but didn't show it at all, he was very stoic and she should of known that. She now felt a little awkward and wanted to make amends for her stupid mistake.

"Don't worry about me Jan, it will turn out one way or the other and I will do what every is necessary to survive it" He looked her in the eye and she tried to return his stare but could not she had to turn away for a moment then back with a smile.

"I am sorry I should of been more tactful please forgive me" she smiled apologetically

He nodded once and returned her slight smile. Looking away from her he stared out of the window again but not at anything in particular then said without moving his stare.

"If you or anyone else you know is visited by anything do not give into it, do not believe it and don't be afraid of it"

"What do you think will come Ray, what can we expect?" she suddenly had a hint of fear but also eagerness in her voice.

"I don't know but just be prepared for something whatever it is, I am not sure what it wants or what the hell it is but just be on your guard"

She nodded and could see he was thinking and calculating things in his mind and she decided to leave him to it. She stood up and said her good bye and shook his hand she wanted to give him a hug but she hesitated and left it for next time maybe, you didn't intrude where Ray didn't want you to, and she didn't want to push anything more today.

She walked away and thought of the man she had just left how unique and strong and fearless he was, she had never met a man like him and knew there was only one. But she had sadness in her heart also, the way he had no choice the way he just had to battle on for his life almost every day and how did he managed to stay sane.

CHAPTER THREE

That evening the night was still and silent, too silent some might say, Bodie was resting and Ray was looking out of the window into the well kept and tidy garden, Darius had gone to bed and the house was once again silent and locked up. Ray had got his car back and was pleased with it the jobs that needed doing were done very well and the car was running perfect. He had restocked it early evening and it was full of petrol and ready to go again. He would normally be off out on the road again by now but was unable to leave until he sorted this problem out, turning back into the room he sat in front of his Ouija board and placed the Planchette on the surface he lightly touched the top and let his mind go blank, instantly there was a slight movement then the pointer moved across the board spelling out something.

ANGELIQUE DARKNESS DANGER

Ray said the words to himself under his breath, there was no more movement from the planchette, but he understood what had been told to him.

"Anything?" Darius asked has he come down for a drink, he went into the kitchen and then came back in with a glass of milk in his hand.

"Angelique, her darkness I suspect" Ray said still looking down at the board in front of him

"She had a darkness that wants to destroy you?"

"Must of released it when Christine died, it must of controlled her when she was ill, or something, we all have a darkness Darius, it's been dormant in Christine now she is dead it has awakened" Ray looked up at Darius and saw concern in his eyes.

"Will you be able to kill it if it is Christine?" he said taking a sip of his milk.

"It isn't her, it is the darkness of Angelique, I do not see it as Christine and this is what it will fail to understand, it has no chance in black hell of making me believe it is her, I know she is gone and in the ground, what remains is pure evil and has to be destroyed"

There was a slight deep and menacing laugh coming from somewhere in the house but where they could not pin point, Bodie pricked his ears up and stood quickly, Darius looked at Ray who was stood silent he was trying to figure out where it was coming from, Darius let out a shout and dropped his milk, which now was black and moving with bright yellow maggots. He stepped away as it smashed on the wooden floor and the thick liquid seemed to move and congeal as the maggots drank it down, he stepped away from it and looked up as the laugh came again loader this time.

"Silly games, don't get agitated" Ray said shaking his head disappointed at the show of power and not impressed one bit. Bodie growled a low growl and looked to the stairs, Ray followed his stare and saw the figure in the shadows it was her again, Angelique, dressed in battle attire and looking straight at them, her eyes piercing black and a look of deranged evil on her face. Darius came next to Ray, he didn't really know why, but it did make him feel safer.

"Oh look at the little brood, all nice and together" she said sarcastically

"You just going to sneak about and talk all day or are you going to tell me what you want?" was Ray's uninterested answer

"I want to rip the beating heart from your chest" she darted her head forward like a viper as she spat the words out at him

"You always talk a lot and throw out threats a lot, gets rather tiring, actions speak louder than words let's see what you are made of bitch, you always did have a high opinion of yourself, a woman thinking she was a man, pathetic"

Darius stood solid he was not sure what Ray was trying to do but he trusted his instinct and kept quiet, he glanced down at Bodie who was poised and ready but staying calm and quiet also, it was down to Ray now to dictate what happened and that suited Darius perfectly.

"It is you who has the high opinion; it is you who is going to be brought down, and sent to hell for the pleasure of the legion that is waiting to take their turn with you"

"You are going to have to be much more original than that, I have heard it all before, and no doubt will hear it all again" Ray was holding steady and not losing the gaze of the black eyes staring at him.

"She was easy to manipulate, she thought she was contacting her "Ray" she was weak just like you all are, they are having a lot of fun with her in the darkness would you like to hear"? She grinned and then turned her gaze to Darius, baring her teeth in an evil smile at him then back to Ray," The beast is to be summoned and it is going to rip you to pieces, nothing can stop it and I will be watching when it tear's you apart"

Bodie walked forward and growled Ray did not stop him so he advanced more and closer, the grin on her face faded and she looked down at the large Dog moving towards her, she backed up and looked at Bodie intensely.

"You won't summon bugger all if my dog rips your fucking throat out now will you?" Ray said, letting Bodie make her feel uncomfortable. She laughed out and turned, she was then gone faster than any of them could see, Bodie ran to where she was, sniffing the floor, but she was now vanished.

"Something wrong here, she is just a facade I think, or she is not what she seems, there is no power there, no strength" Ray said to no one in particular

"What is she waiting for, or who?" Darius said.

"I don't know but we will find out I am sure, playing games, testing, whatever she is doing she is waiting for something or someone like you say, maybe to give her strength or power".

"Have you come across this sort of thing before?"

"Not really, but is it not what I have experienced, it is what I feel, the vibes I get for them and this one seems strange I can't put my finger on it"

"Maybe because of whom she is and the connection you had with her?"

"I never really liked the Angelique side to be honest; we will see what happens with it"

"You need to rest Ray, have a break, you can't just keep going on and on without some time to recuperate every now and then."

"They never rest, I can never rest, you can't just turn it off"

"I know that, but while you have the chance you should take some time to recharge, refresh, just rest a while nothing wrong with that, eat properly, sleep properly have some down time at least" Darius didn't talk like this often and was surprised he was now, but, he was genuinely concerned for his friend and wanted to get it across anyway he could without offending or sounding ridiculous.

"More importantly be aware if anything visits you Darius to not be afraid of it and don't believe anything it says to you, it isn't Christine here, no matter what it looks or sounds like no matter what it says or asks of you, so be diligent"

"I will, I understand" Darius said as he picked up the broken pieces of glass and took them into the kitchen only to return with a cloth to wipe up the spilt milk. (which now only looked like spilt milk?)

Bodie walked calmly back to where Ray was standing, who reached down and stroked his large head and they both went into the kitchen.

Ray returned five minutes later with a large mug of tea and a packet of biscuits. He and Bodie sat in front of the TV as he flicked through the channels seeming unconcerned at this time; Darius left them in peace and went to bed, he had concerns but he saw Ray was not too bothered, so trusted his instinct, when Ray looked concerned he would also be concerned.

What Darius didn't realise was Ray was very stoic, he would show patience and endurance in the face of adversity, he knew there was danger here, but until it really showed its self he was not going to get upset about it. To some it might seem like he was being nonchalant but until his gut instinct told him there was imminent danger he was going to stay calm, danger would come, that is for sure but it was not here yet, she was not powerful enough and was just playing silly games as he put it. To the untrained eye to the unknowing or the nervous this might seem a strong show of the supernatural or evil spirit but to Ray, who had seen much more than most, it was not a threat, but he knew all this was leading into something it was just a matter of getting more pieces of the puzzle, she was waiting or hoping for something but what it was he didn't know. He would worry about it when t happened.

He flicked through the channels and was not impressed with anything that was on, he didn't watch TV much and seeing the quality of the programs he didn't mind missing it. He turned the set off and sat in silence, he listened to it because silence was his friend, Bodie laid with his head on his paws and sat with his master. To some it might seem strange, to others it might seem like a form of meditation, to Ray it helped him think, to de stress, to relax. He had always liked his own company and could not stand noise or noisy people, he sipped his tea, he dunked his biscuits and took deep breaths. Over an hour passed and he let Bodie out the back door so he could go patrol and do what he had to do, Ray washed his pot up and when Bodie came back in they locked up and went up to bed.

Jan was up early and on her way into town she had taken some time off work while Ray was around, she wanted to see more of him but was not sure how to do it without seeming to pushy or looking desperate or insensitive even. She was going to use the excuse of asking Darius to get her some ammunition for her browning 9mm hand gun which was illegal and she risked imprisonment if she was every discovered with it. Darius had many contacts legal and illegal and he was able to obtain the ammunition for her, she found the risk a little exciting and wanted some practice in any way she use to drive to an abandoned quarry and practice with her weapon she was going to ask if Ray wanted to join her but knew he wouldn't. She had lost some weight since the last time she had met Ray, She helped him with Xander and she would help him again here if he needed it. The running was hard to begin with but she stuck with t and it had become the

norm now to run most days and it had done her mind and body a world of good, she felt good and was much fitter and more active. After her visit into town she drove to Darius's house she checked her face in the mirror, just a little make up not too much, taking deep breaths she turned into the long drive and headed to the house. Checking her face one last time in the mirror she got out of the car and as casual as she could walk to the front door. Knocking hard she waited and sighed to herself as Ray answered he was just in jeans and had obviously just got out of the shower and had a shave he looked a fine sight for her eyes topless and his piercing blue eyes fixed on hers, a smile came across his face and she actually felt a weakness in her knees.

"Jan, how are you, is all ok?" he said friendly and in a matter of fact manner.

It took her off guard for a moment she was not use to him looking and sounding normal, she smiled and cleared her throat before answering.

"Yes, yes fine, I am here to see Darius, is he around?"

"No he has gone to open his shop in town, is it important, you can ring him there" Ray smiled again and he looked her straight in the eye, he instantly knew she had an attraction for him and he didn't want to put her in any awkward situation he stood aside and gestured her inside. She smiled and came past him meaningfully brushing against his large powerful chest as she did she went in and then turned to face him.

"Fancy a brew? " Ray asked has he shut the door and headed for the kitchen.

"No thanks, I am not imposing or anything am I?"

"No. Don't be silly" looking out of the open back door he checked on Bodie who was laid out on the lawn enjoying the fresh air and warm weather.

"He looks happy enough" she smiled standing next to him; she could smell the fresh smell of the shower he had just had, and feel his strength just standing next to her.

"Yeah it is good to give him a break every now and then, he likes to sun bathe after a good shower he was rather dirty and he takes some washing" Ray smiled at her and they locked eyes for a moment until she pulled away almost like a love struck school girl.

"What about you, don't you like a bit of a soak in the sun?"

"No not really, I prefer the shade myself, shall we go sit down" he walked off into the living room and sat on the sofa; Jan followed and sat next to him but not to close.

"You are looking very fit Jan, have you been working out I seem to remember you being larger before?" Ray said with all the tact he was blessed with.

"I run a lot now, lost several stone and toned up a lot, feel much better for it and I keep running at least three times a week so yeah, and thank you" she smiled at him

"Excellent, it's doing you a lot of good, too many people start things and don't finish them, a bit of will power and determination is what is needed"

"Very true, you keep fit Ray, mind I suppose you have too" she looked at his muscular body and saw the many scars that were across it, wondering what had caused them and what fights and battles he had been in to get so many.

"I would be in a lot of trouble in fact I wouldn't be here now if I didn't" he stretched back and sighed out she noticed a slight twinge has he lifted his right arm.

"You a bit stiff there?" she innocently said looking at his right shoulder.

"Didn't know you could tell in these jeans" he said smiling and being totally relaxed

"Silly bugger" she shook her head, but loved it, let me look at your shoulder, she leaned forward and put her hands on his neck then down to his shoulder and across his back. Loving the touch of his skin but she also felt the knots and tension of his muscle. She gestured him to turn away from her and she started to massage his right shoulder and back. Rubbing her finger in just at the right pressure, then circling her hands it felt good and Ray let her continue she was good at this and he was not going to complain. She worked her hands over his powerful shoulders and back.

"You should be laid flat really but I hope this helps" she said continuing to massage him.

Ray stood up and without saying a word he laid face down flat on the floor, Jan eagerly knelt beside him and carried on running her soothing hands over his back and shoulders, he had his arms folded and his head resting on them, letting out a slight pleasing moan every now and then has her hands moved over his back and shoulders. She was turning herself on and just wanted to pounce on him, it was difficult for her to concentrate on what she was doing.

"You are good at this; it feels relaxing what else can you do?" Ray said without too much emotion in his voice and she was a little taken off guard, he seemed totally relaxed and didn't seem to have a care in the world and was he actually flirting with her?

"You would be surprised what I can do" she said running her full palms all over his back, the professional massage had stopped it was just sexual feeling and touching and rubbing now.

"I bet I would, shame the circumstances are not different"

This deflated her a little but she did not stop, she carried on and moved her hands boldly to his lower back and over his arse then back up, she wanted him and wanted him to grab and ravish her here and now, he breathing was heavier and her excitement was rising every second, she ran her hand through his hair and down across his shoulders, he then turned round and laid on his back, he looked at her, she could just detect a very slight smile on his lips, she was not going to give up this chance and carried on massaging his shoulders and down his chest, she pushed at his muscular stomach, looking at the scars she ran her fingers over them wanting to follow with her mouth and lips but dare not for fear of rejection. She was at the top of his jeans, she so wanted to undo his belt rip open them jeans and delve down deeper. He reached out and touched her hair gently stroking it and then twisting his fist taking a hand full and pulling her down to his lips they kissed slightly then deeply. She melted at his strong mouth his commanding way and she kissed him deeply back, never wanting it to end. They were locked in an embrace and their mouths joined. Then pulling away he looked her deep in the eye and tilted her head back by pulling her hair, she found the gesture and control stimulating and exciting.

She looked back at him and wanted him to take her there and then, ravish her, make her his, she would welcome anything he wanted to do to her.

"What do you want Jan?" he said

"You know what I want, always have every since I first saw you" her shyness and nervousness had gone she was not going to lie, she was not going to be bashful, she wanted him and she was going to tell him, she had gone past that threshold now and lust had taken over her emotions.

The next hour and half was the best sex she had ever experienced, sometimes loving sometimes rough sometimes just animalistic but she loved every second of it, and never in her wildest dreams did she think she would ever be in this position of making love and having sex with Ray Sibson. She gave herself completely and there were no inhibitions she knew he wanted it all and he took it and she let him gladly and enjoyed it immensely, in a way he needed her, a release an outlet a pressure valve, a let off of steam and pent up energy. Nothing was said and nothing needed to be said. They lay in each other's arms on the floor naked and she stroked his chest with her fingers and felt satisfied and relaxed, no shame no regret just pleasure and satisfaction.

Bodie cautiously trotted in and looked at them both for a few seconds he turned and went back out Ray smiled at him and watched him go.

"Fancy a brew?" he said looking back at Jan who smiled and nodded a yes, Ray stood up put his jeans on and went into the kitchen Jan got dressed and sat waiting on the sofa, not really believing what had just happened, it was something she wanted to happen she, was just so surprised it had. Trying to do something with her hair she stopped has Ray come in with a mug of tea for her.

"Sorry there is no biscuits someone ate them all last night" he said innocently

"I will bring some next time" she said taking a sip of her tea.

He sat next to her and they each had a drink, he looked at her and she smiled back at him.

"Bet you think I am a right tart now?" she said half jokingly

"Yep" he said joking back with a smile

"Bastard" she said taking a sip of her tea but smiling.

"I think you are alright Jan, and I am glad you called round"

"Well thank you, I suppose from you that is bloody good compliment"

"It is yes, I don't just drop my pants for anyone you know"

"Oh shut up, you silly arse, and drink your tea"

They both laughed and the atmosphere was relaxed and comfortable they chatted for a while and when Jan left sometime later, they both felt good. It had been a very productive visit for her and she found herself smiling as she drove home, she did however call into see Darius at his shop and tell him she needed some 9mm bullets for her Beretta hand gun.

Ray spent the rest of the day happy, he played ball with Bodie and they actually had time to toy fight something they had not done for a long time. It did them both the world of good and took them away from the situation for a time and allowed them to forget, just for a short while and live and feel like normal beings. This break was like a breath of fresh air for them both a little short time in Eden and time to heal to refresh and time to enjoy. Ray knew it would not last but he was going to take it and make sure Bodie and he got out of it whatever they could, while they could. The eye of the storm it maybe because he knew something was coming, but right now was time to enjoy and take a break.

Darius Returned that evening and found Ray watching a film on the TV, he seemed very relaxed and calm, he had no lament or regret what he had done with Jan, you only live once was his thinking and she handed it to him on a plate, he took it and eat it and digested it. He didn't really look up when Darius came in, he did grunt a greeting has Darius said hello. Bodie looked to be out for the count laid on the carpet in front of the TV. Darius was tired and went up to bed, he and Jan had, had a talk earlier and thought Ray was doing the right thing by relaxing somewhat, but they were both concerned about the circumstances. Jan was going to a coven of her sisters that night and discus what they could do, and the situation. The night air was crisp and fresh, Ray stood out under the clear sky looking up at the stars, sometime later, and Bodie was walking round the garden sniffing everything that looked interesting. The vastness of the universe was out there and Ray was looking out towards it, it was a still beautiful night, he liked the crisp air and the silence of it all. He felt good and had no strange or bad feeling which in a way was strange. But he felt nothing threatening no presence of darkness. He took deep breaths and slowly eased them back out. His head was clear and his mind settled. He was coming to terms of Christine being gone for good but there was this matter of Angelique to sort out. When he finds out what she is after, he will deal with it, but as of yet he had no idea so was not going to let it worry him. Even though his board had warned him of the danger he would react to an action rather than go looking for it. He strolled round the garden alone with is thoughts and at peace with himself, Bodie sniffed about and marked his spot several times. Darius was looking out of his bed room window down at them he had awoke and was conscious someone was outside when he saw it was Ray he watched for a short while, watching him walking round the large lawn and garden wondering what he was thinking about and what he was going to do. Turning he looked round his own room for a moment then went back into bed, his day had been busy and he was tired. Ray would be back in when he was ready he thought.

Jan had been out with the sisters most of the night they had been discussing Ray and the situation, their discussions always were fruitful and interesting. She had been and was still thinking about her time with him, He needs a woman, who knows him thru and thru and will give him ease when he needs it, not expecting anything else. She knows he needs her and it is enough. She is glad to be able to help him with this. It is her love for him and respect for what and who he is that makes this arrangement possible. She had no misconceptions that he would be gone when all this was over she may not see him again for some years, but at least she now had this bond with him, this time and experience. Something to remember and something to cherish. She had gone to bed and laid there in silence and the dark, taking deep breaths she closed her eyes and thought and wondered what Ray would be doing right at this moment, would he be asleep or would he be awake and up?.

Ray was actually looking at an article in a news paper about some disappearances from the Sunnycliffe woods. They were not too far from where Darius lived, and his instinct told him there was something very wrong, he read the article and knew the place must be cursed or something was there. He decided to pay the woods a visit the next day with Bodie and have a walk round the place to see what vibes he got and the feeling it gave him. He went to bed and slept well, no nightmares last night and he had none this night he slept full and solid. Darius was having breakfast when he came down the next morning he went into the kitchen and let Bodie out into the back Garden.

"What are you going to do today?" Darius asked has he ate his serial

"Today I am going to a place called Sunnycliffe woods" Ray almost announced proudly, while he filled the kettle up with water. Darius stopped eating and slowly looked up.

"It is said to be an evil place, strange things have happened there in the past, people go missing, sightings, and lots of strange things, why are you going there?"

"You have just said why I am going there" Ray got himself a mug and dropped a tea bag into it; he went to the fridge and took some milk out.

"Have you had a sign, a signal, something drawing you there?" Darius continued to eat his breakfast but was looking at Ray.

"No, just read an article in a paper last night, there are a lot of strange stories surrounding the place just thought I would take a look" he stood waiting for the water in the kettle to boil.

"It will take you about half an hour to get there, be careful there is some presence there that is for sure, but what it is I have no idea"

"It will be a run out if nothing else, keep it in mind for future reference, anyway I need the exercise, give Bodie a roam"

"Be careful and be on your guard" Darius finished his cereal and stood up, putting the bowl and spoon into the dishwasher.

"Got anymore biscuits anywhere?" Ray asked looking in the cupboard above the wok top.

"No someone ate them all; you will have to get yourself some on the way today"

Darius said his goodbye and left for his shop, Ray made his tea and looked for some eggs for his breakfast; he made some scrambled ones and made Bodie some too.

It was around lunch time they set off and drove to Sunnycliffe woods, Ray was curious about the place and wanted to see it and walk round it, he drove steady and felt the car was running well the mechanic had done a good job. He put her through her paces speeding up testing the brakes, listening to the engine, testing the steering the feel of the car and the sound of it, he liked the way it was running. They pulled up slowly and parked just off the road way by a wooden sign screwed into a tree stating they had arrived at Sunnycliffe woods, and stating it was a public footpath with a wooden arrow pointing the way. They both got out and Bodie stood sniffing the air, he sniffed the ground and walked a little way in, Ray locked his car and followed. It was quiet and a very beautiful place, trees were on all sides but the path was wide and well used. They strolled on and enjoyed the peace and quiet, the air had that woodland smell and was very pleasing to them, and Bodie ran on and explored like he always did but always kept his master in sight. It didn't take long before Ray's instincts stirred and he felt the danger, the hidden darkness that was there. Bodie came close as he felt it also. Something was not right here, it looked lovely, it looked safe and it looked just like any other beauty spot but there was a lurking menace, a concealed darkness. He stopped and looked round, looking for clues, looking for signs. But he could not find any, Bodie sniffed the ground and they both carried on walking slowly and looking and scoping all the time. The path wound into the thick wooded area and forked off, Ray took the left one it just seemed to him the stronger pull, so he followed it. Rising up past a felled decaying tree he took large strides up the incline and across to where it levelled out again, the path was narrower here and he stopped for a moment. Looking at the growth round the area, it all looked natural but the closer he looked, the closer he inspected he could see it was just a little too thick in places, he walked to such a place and Bodie stood growling low has he sensed it, Ray was instantly on guard he looked round and checked his back and area round him. It was silent and still, there could have been no one else on earth at that moment the ears strained to hear something but there was nothing there. Usually he would like it here but this was different, it was a bad place, an evil was here but he was not sure where. His instincts were high and he felt the emanating darkness around the place, not many would feel it or see it, but he did, but he also could see and understand why it would be undetected by anyone else. He kicked at the shrubbery and then noticed it, marks on the ground, not animal marks like a badger or fox, no, these were different marks. He kicked at the shrubbery again and it was too tight too solid, he looked round once again then leaned down pulling at the woven twigs and greenery, he pulled and it moved slightly, he pulled again in a different direction and it gave slightly, it was a hatch, a doorway of sorts. He lifted the growth and it moved exposing a hole, a purpose dug hole, and a well kept and maintained one too, Bodie came forward and sniffed the smell that came up, it was not very pleasant. He growled and backed off his hair lifted on his back. Ray let the hatch fall shut and backed off, it was not big enough for him to get down anyway. He took a deep breath and walked back, as he did he looked around again and spotted a few more alterations in the growth on his way and knew there were more hatches. Well at least his hunch was right, something was here, and living under ground, something sinister. He walked back and Bodie followed. He passed a large birch tree and walked under it and on his way. High up in this tree were two piercing eyes watching him. They had spotted him earlier and had kept looking at him all the way to the hatch and back and was now watching him head away again. She was crouched on a large branch and partly hidden; she stood up and watched Ray and Bodie head off out of sight. Baring her teeth Angelique hissed at them with hate in her eyes, but a devilish smile on her face too as she stood in silence watching where they had gone.

CHAPTER FOUR

Driving back after walking round the place for another half hour, Ray was in thought, he knew the place was evil and that there was something lurking but he didn't know what. The trap doors where not that big but still something the size of a small man would be able to get down there, or a light framed woman, maybe a coven of witches living under ground? He would consult his board, strange nothing had been said about the place before. People reported missing, but why have the police not found anything especially if they had dogs? He found the tunnel pretty quickly, but then again he knew what he was looking for and had the experience of hunting things like this, they would take their victims, clean the area and then transport them to a tunnel which would be far away from where they originally attacked. Thinking more about it he was working his mind and trying to decide what would be lurking in the tunnels, and then he shook his head. He still had the problem of Angelique to sort out so it could wait; he locked the information away and would use it for future reference. Calling in at a shop on the way back he purchased himself several packets of biscuits and some dog food for Bodie then headed home. It didn't take him long and he came back just in time to hear the phone ringing, he opened the door and dashed for the phone in the hall way picking it up.

"Yes" he said bluntly.

"Ray? Its Jan, hope I am not disturbing you, but I have found something in my garden they look like small animal foot prints never seen them before, if you send me your phone number I will send you a photo of them to see what you think"

"How many, describe them to me and how they are positioned" Ray said unalarmed.

"Well it's like a small man has ran across the soil and there is a hand print too, small like a child's but the feet are a funny shape it is very confusing"

"Something moving or bounding along like a monkey, every now and then putting its hand down to propel its self along do you think?"

"Yes, yes I see what you mean I have seen them do that on the TV, how did you know?"

"Just a guess, have you heard anything or seen anything else?"

"No, no nothing, what is it, do you know?"

"Jan gather your things and come here, can you do that. Is it possible for you to stay here for a while, bring what you need and let Darius know, I would prefer everyone together instead of spread about it obviously knows about you, the situation will be easier to control if we are together I feel, looks like people, places are being watched or checked out"

"Yes of course, I will sort my stuff out and arrange cover for my work; I will be over this evening"

Ray hung up the phone and thought for a moment stood silent and still thoughts running through his mind and he let out a sigh, Bodie came in and Ray shut the door they walked into the kitchen and the kettle was switched on ready to make a brew.

Darius and Jan more or less came arrived at the house together Jan had an overnight bag and a large suit case too. They talked for a little while has they locked their vehicles before entering the house; Bodie came to see who it was when the front door opened. He looked and then walked away back into the house, Darius was carrying Jan's large case with a little difficulty when he had offered he did not realise it might give him a hernia, what the hell she had in there he didn't know but was glad to put it down in the living room, they both came in and watched Ray, who was topless and he was doing press ups on the living room floor, he seemed oblivious to them being there but he knew they were.

Darius left him to it and went up stairs for a shower, Jan watched for a little while and then strolled into the kitchen and made herself a drink. When she came back in she saw Ray was now doing sit ups and again she watched him. Her thoughts were not totally clean but she was entitled to her own thoughts so had not shame.

He was a powerful man and a fit one, she quietly sat down on a chair trying to act normal but wanting to pounce on him at any moment. He excited her and she would never forget the passion they had shared, whether it would happen again she didn't know but hoped it would.

Darius came back down about ten minutes later after his quick shower and glanced over at Jan still watching Ray still doing sit ups, his abdominal strength was dominant and it showed in his muscle body, he kept himself fit, he had too. He walked into the kitchen, Jan looked up for a moment then back down at Ray who had stopped and was stretched out on the carpet. Breathing deep he sat up looking at Jan, who smiled at him.

"You are very fit" she said looking at his strong chest and shoulders.

"Fit to drop" he said half joking, standing up he stretched out his body and breathed back out again has he relaxed.

"Did you find anything today, at the woods?" Darius asked walking into the room.

"It is an evil place alright; there is something there, tunnels and concealed entrances, not a nice place to be I would say"

"Thought so, strange things have happened there over the years"

"Where is this?" Jan asked feeling a little left out of the conversation

"Sunnycliffe woods, it's a beauty spot not too far away" Darius said to her.

"I know it yeah, dark place, always has been I am surprised something had not been done about it before today" she settled back into the chair and suddenly felt how tired she felt.

"Well something is there and I will pay it a visit in due time no doubt but we have other matters at hand, Tell me about these prints" he said looking at Jan"

This morning, not sure how long they have been there though?"

"Prints, what are we talking about?" Darius asked sitting on the settee looking over at Jan.

"Jan has discovered some strange foot marks in her garden, something small, might be nothing of course but I feel it is something, more importantly is that whatever it is, knows about Jan, so will probably know about everyone else. If Angelique knows then what ever she has with her knows, that is why I asked her to come and stay here" Ray said looking at Darius

"Right, I see, I was wondering what all this was about?" he nodded and was now pleased he understood why she had turned up with suitcase in hand.

"I am starving, anyone fancy an Indian take away, my treat" Jan said smiling at them both. The absolute disgusted look on Ray's face told her without a doubt it was a "no" Darius smiled to himself knowing Ray detested the food and what his reaction would be.

"I will pass thanks Jan" Darius said politely

"Disgusting slop how the hell anyone can eat that shit is beyond me" Ray said walking into the Kitchen, Jan was a little taken back and looked at Darius who was smiling and put his hand up to calm her before she got upset.

"Offer him Fish and chips, Jan, he will bite your hand off" Darius whispered leaning forward toward her with a wink of his eye.

"Fish and chips then?" she shouted towards the kitchen area.

"And mushy peas, thank you" Ray's voice came back, Darius laughed and nodded he would have the same has Jan stood up and went out for the food.

Darius came into the kitchen and saw Ray staring out into the back garden, he seemed deep in thought but at ease.

"What is going to happen Ray have you any idea?" he asked standing next to him.

"That place bothers me, and these tracks Jan has found, something small, something moving in a crouched manner, probably, she found a hand print by the foot prints, that to me suggests something moving like a primate, one two legs but sometimes on all fours?"

"Yeah, like a chimpanzee does you mean?"

"Yes, I found tunnels in the woods today, not large enough for a full grown man but large enough for a small framed one or a woman" he shook his head has he was thinking.

"You putting two and two together, and coming up with the answer?" Darius asked

"Well it is a distance away but it is possible I suppose, Angelique is up to something and what it is we will find out, but it seems she is not strong enough on her own, or she would of attacked by now don't you think?" he turned to face Darius who looked him back and nodded his head in agreement.

"Maybe, or she just likes to play games, toying with us, messing and seeing if we buckle under when she comes, testing the water sort of speak"

Ray folded his arms and lifted his left hand up to his mouth and started to bite his thumb nail.

"Is that a sign of nerves?" Darius asked half joking

"No, but no one else will bite them for me" Ray smiled and leaned over to flick the electric kettle on; he wanted a tea with his fish and chips.

"Your face was a picture when she asked about Indian food" Darius laughed and giggled to himself has he thought about it.

"Bloody horrid stuff looks like dog shite doesn't it, smells like it too how the hell people can eat that is beyond me" Ray shook his head in disgust.

"Some people love it, each to their own eh?"

"What is wrong with good old English food, don't need this foreign muck"

"Well it's the world we live in, different cultures integrate and people try new things, not everyone likes English food", each to their own"

"Slop, it's disgusting, no idea what the hell is in for a start" Ray raised his voice just that bit and Darius knew it was pointless arguing. He left it and got some plates out ready for when Jan returned with the food, English food.

Ray went and put a shirt on and made sure Bodie had some fresh water down, and also fed him two tins of the food he had bought earlier from the shop. Bodie welcomed it and devoured them with no problem.

Jan returned soon and they all eat the English food she had bought for them, it was welcomed as they were all ready for something to eat. After clearing up and Jan had a shower the night had dropped in, it was dark outside and quiet. Bodie was laid at Ray's feet, who himself was slouched in a large leather chair; Jan sat on the settee with Darius. It was silent for a while as they relaxed, but then Bodie sat up, not too quickly but fast enough to spring Ray into alert mode. He watched his dog, Bodies ears pricked up and he was looking at the back door through the kitchen. Ray waited and listened.

"What is it?" Jan asked, Ray put his hand up to her to signal silence, none of them could hear anything but Bodie could he moved slowly to the kitchen area, quietly followed by Ray who took out a hunting knife from his bag he had on the side, he held it in his right hand has he slowly followed his dog, a low growl came from Bodie which was enough for Ray to know danger was imminent. Darius was behind them and asked quietly.

"Do I put the lights on; it illuminates the whole back garden?"

"Do it, when I say" Ray said standing by the back door, Darius went to the switch that turned the back and garden lights on, Jan stayed back in the living room, her heart was going faster but she was in control, and knew what she was doing.

Ray looked intense, he was taking his lead from Bodie slowly and quietly he turned the key and unlocked the door he could hear the noise outside now too, Bodie tilted his head slightly trying to catch the movements of them outside, he crouched and his growl became deeper, Ray took as the signal and nodded to Darius, who flicked the switch at the same time Ray opened the door and they borh dashed out.

The garden was bright has the powerful lights awoke and shone brightly, showing Bodie fighting with a creature and Ray wrestling with two more, Angelique was stood back watching and enjoying what she was seeing. Jan came forward from the room and stood with Darius watching out into the arena that was the garden as the fight raged, these creatures were small but powerful and vicious they seemed to take command from Angelique and she was enjoying the power, laughing and snarling as they fought in front of her, a fourth creature was crouched beside her and ready to pounce into the fight at her command.

Jan looked away it was a nasty fight and she watched as Ray was in his most brutal battle mode a necessity but disturbing sight, she had witnessed it before some years ago but to see it live again in front her was more sickening than she had remembered. Bodie ripped at the vile creature and pinned it to the ground snapping and snarling at it ripping and biting at its throat eventually getting the better of it. Ray threw one of the creatures off and hurled it away his knife sticking into the second one. They were the dwellers from the forest and now under Angelique's command, fighters and scavengers they were without mercy or pity and would kill anything in front of them or die trying. Vile looking things with sharpened teeth, long scratching claws and powerful bodies that were strong and hard as steel. They fought like mad insane creatures, what they lacked in height and technique they more and made up with brute strength and determination to kill. Ray stabbed the one with him hard and fast over and over he knew he had this one down, the other was racing back at him now but dramatically taken in mid air as Bodie timed his jump perfectly as usual and brought it crashing down to the ground both Bodie and Ray pounced and destroyed and killed the creature within seconds they both stood and looked at Angelique who's face had turned to anger and hate. The creature with her howled for its dead comrades and spat and snarled at them both eager to dash forward but being held back by its new master.

Ray looked Angelique in the eye and hated every inch of her, she was now marked for death and as soon as possible in his book. She shook her head and was gone, followed by her new found servant. The night swallowed them and it was again silent. Ray took a deep breath he was not harmed just a few scratches Bodie walked over to the two dead creatures and sniffed at them, he knew they were dead.

Darius and Jan came out and looked in disgust at what lay dead on the grass in front of them, they had never seen such ugly vile looking creatures. nothing about them said anything nice or appealing they were just pure evil and dark.

"Too easy" Ray said looking at Darius.

"Another test do you think seeing what you are capable of?"

"Tomorrow I will go to where they are and burn them out, the fucking lot of them we are sitting ducks here, I won't just sit here and let them come as and when, I will go there and destroy her it must be what I found in that forest "

You don't know how many there are, what are we doing with these?" Darius looked at the dead bodies on his lawn.

"Burn them, do it now and keep an eye out for more there is a lot of these things I am guessing so be careful, let's get it done"

Without another word the bodies were dragged to the far side of the house and petrol poured over them, they soon had a fire going with some fallen tree branches and bits of wood Darius had laying about the creatures burned well their oily dirty bodies smelling vile, the smoke rose high into the night sky but was hidden by the cover of darkness, the fire raged for some time the burning bodies going through several stages as the flames engulfed them burning melting and destroying the evidence, Ray stayed with it and used a long stick to keep the fire going and made sure the bodies were fully gone beyond recognition. He left them smouldering and went in several hours later. They could dispose of the rest the next day, he looked round and watched for anything unusual, he was surprised they had not reappeared at all. Darius cleared up some of the mess and they went back in, Ray took a shower to get the smell of the fire and stench of the burning bodies off his own and out of his hair.

It was early morning before they had done and the sun would be up soon, Jan made some tea and they sat in silence for a short while.

Quietly and stealthy the fourth creature came out from its hiding place, it was an expert at watching and observing without being noticed. It kept close to the ground crawling on its belly to where the fire was smouldering, taking the small container from under its ragged top which Angelique had given to it. Carefully shifting through the chard and burned remains it took some flesh, a tooth, some bone and put them into the container, making small grunting noises as it did and its shifty eyes looking all round as it went about collecting the bits of body parts from its dead colleagues. When the container was full it backed off looking round as it did all the time and was silently gone without anyone noticing it had been there at all, something it was very good at.

The daylight came and the sun slowly rose in the sky getting stronger and hotter as it awoke the world it was shining down on.

Ray and Darius were up early and burying the remains from the fire, they dug it down a few feet and made sure it was all gone the packed the soil on top leaving no evidence except for the fresh soil on top which would settle and Darius would sow grass over and there would be no trace left at all, no one would know it would just be another place Ray had disposed of something, they were all over the country and only he knew where.

Jan made them breakfast for when they had come back in, the excitement of it all had turned to a slight fear now, the battle and killing of last night the way Ray turned on the warrior in him and became a different person then seemed to just switch back, it was not that she didn't know or understand but it was just something she found frightening and a little disturbing, she surprised herself with her feelings but knew she would have to be there no matter what happened if she was needed.

After breakfast Darius rang his good friend little John someone who had helped them in the past and someone Darius had helped many time to get his life back together, he was a huge and powerful man and a superior ally to have in any situation, he knew Ray and Ray knew him so there would be no friction there, Ray would need all the help he could get and he knew it, he had no idea how many of the dwellers there was and he needed someone he could trust and someone he knew, little John would fit that description just fine.

Jan washed up and cleared up then she went to her bag and took out a large wooded case she placed it on the table and opened it, inside was her gun.

A Beretta 92FS, 9 millimetre semi automatic pistol, she looked at it with loving eyes and slowly lifted it from its velvet encasing, she held the hand gun in her hand and gripped the handle, the black non glare Bruniton finish made it look a formidable weapon, which indeed it was, and she knew how to use it.

"Where the hell did you get that thing from anyway?" Ray asked looking at her from the kitchen door way.

"I have a very special friend in America who arranged a very special shipment for me "she said not taking her eyes off the weapon.

"Well I have seen you use that and am impressed, just be bloody careful all the same" Ray said half jokingly but with a serious tone he didn't want any stray bullets ending up in him or Bodie if anything happened here again.

"I have a twenty round magazine with it, I always hit what I aim at, and I have a four point nine inch barrel, I have an open slide design, this virtually eliminates jamming, also an internal firing pin block system, it only moves when the trigger is pulled, she is semiautomatic double and single action, a very beautiful lady indeed"

"Yes I am sure, and totally illegal as well, you are one hell of a woman Jan hell of a woman" She almost lovingly looked at her gun and carefully placed it back down on the table, she took out the two magazines from there cut out slots in the box and then took a box of bullets from her bag and began to load these into the magazines one at a time. Ray had to smile and left her to it, he admired her admiration for the weapon and he had seen her use it before so knew it was not wasted on her, it was just so out of character for a doctor like herself to carry and own such a piece of hardware.

Darius had to go out for a while Bodie patrolled the grounds most of the day keeping guard and Ray got his knives and petrol bombs ready he made these filling bottles with petrol and attaching a rag to the top, it was something he had used before and it was effective he wanted to burn them out and hopefully roast a lot of them down in their lair. He had no idea how big the underground catacombs would be but he wanted to do something and getting some of them would be better than none at all he was a sitting duck here, specially now Angelique had a new found army to command.

Darius came back and told Ray little John would be around later if he needed him, he was glad to help in anyway, Ray nodded and kept it in mind he knew a powerful faithful man like Little John was always good to have around.

The rest of the day went by easily they were all ready and it was just a matter of picking the right time to head off, Ray wanted it quiet so was thinking late evening the cover of darkness would be a blessing but also a danger, they knew the place much better than he did but he was going to hit them as hard as he could and hope he would have the element of surprise on his said. He had considered taking Jan with him she could pick quite a few off with her Berretta but he decided against it, too dangerous for her and he didn't want the added distraction of having to keep an eye out for her there. He was ready and it was just a matter of waiting for the right time to set off.

The night in the forest was darker than normal, a little fire was burning. Angelique was crouched over it, she had something in her hand, a powder? She was chanting over the fire, throwing the powder into it, the flames danced a strange dance, more straight, more defined and much slower, the fire seemed to be in slow motion, several of the forest dwellers were sat behind her, watching obediently.

"The crushed bones of our comrades, the flesh of the warriors, the tooth of the dark ones, we ask thee to accept them as a token of our loyalty, we need the fallen warriors of last night to be avenged, we need the white beast of hell to finally come and finish this vile creature that has caused us so much agony and pain over the years, only the mighty white beast can destroy him, send the white beast to do what has to be done"

She threw more of the crushed powdered bone and flesh of the dead dwellers into the fire it made the fire slow even more and almost stand still in motion.

The dwellers all stirred and looked at each other with a worried look something was feeling wrong, something was happening they could sense it in the air; Angelique was motionless like in a trace the fire had stopped moving and seemed in stopped animation. They shifted and looked round at each other, grunting and sniffing the air as they did, something was happening and they didn't understand what, they began to shift about and panic looking round to try and see what was causing their fear. The fire suddenly roared up like a massive explosion and settle back down again to as it was, Angelique smiled and lifted her arms up and out to the sky mumbling a spell, she stood up and looked at her anxious dwellers she opened her arms and turned her palms upwards smiling at them she said.

"It is done, we must get there to watch the slaughter, the great white beast has been summoned and cannot return to hell unless it kills its prey, come, let's not miss any of it, she dashed off and was followed by several of the dwellers, the rest just danced around and rejoiced but they were not sure of what they were actually rejoicing yet.

They moved fast and ran at speed, the night had dropped in and was cool the moon was out and the sky clear, they ran side by side, keeping out of sight as much as they could, Angelique had a grin on her face and laughed as she heard the distant howl, she barked a laugh out in total uncontrolled excitement. The howl was hollow but each time it sounded it was stronger and getting nearer. It made them run faster and more eager to get to where the slaughter would commence.

CHAPTER FIVE

It was Bodie who again alerted everyone; he got up and looked at Ray, who was in his jacket and ready to set off. Ray stood silent and listened. Bodie's hair lifted on his back, he went to the back door and Ray slowly opened it for him. The lights were already on and they could see the whole area pretty well.

"What is it, is she back?" Jan asked coming into the kitchen followed by Darius, they all stood and listened, Ray looking at Bodie. It was silent and they strained their ears but Bodie stepped out and growled, he heard it first and it bothered him tremendously, Ray sensed the dogs unease and knew something was coming.

"Get inside and lock the doors" Ray said without looking at them, he too stepped out and stood with his dog.

"Little John is on his way" Darius said to Jan as they closed the door and locked it, then went to the window to peer out, their fear growing.

The distant howl seemed to be coming for all directions, like a wolf, but much more powerful and lower in tone, Bodie looked up at Ray, he knew this was something bad, and Ray touched the dogs head and knelt down, putting his arms round Bodies powerful neck and hugged him close. Jan watched as they embraced for a few seconds she was touched and could feel a lump rising in her throat, what she knew of Ray Sibson, the fearless warrior the man of steel, she knew what she was now witnessing was something extremely serious and rare, it was like they were saying goodbye to each other just in case they didn't make it. She looked at Darius and he looked back at her with the same fear in his eyes. They didn't have to say anything, they both could feel the danger and it petrified them.

The howl was louder and closer, whatever it was, it was gaining distance fast, Ray looked up at the full moon, it was glaring down like a spot light to a gladiatorial arena, well if he was to die at least it would be under a spot light.

Angelique arrived out of breath and gasping for air the two dwellers by her side seemed fresh and unhurried they were use to long runs and very fit. They quietly peered from the trees at the far side of the garden, hidden and out of sight they could see Ray with Bodie in the garden they could see the two faces looking out of the kitchen window and they could sense the urgency and the electric atmosphere all round the place. She rubbed her hands together and breathed heavy, she was going to enjoy every minute of this. She crouched and took deep breaths she was calming and her heart rate coming back down. She looked up at the moon and then smiled as she heard the white beast howl once again, it was close and it was getting closer all the time.

Ray stood up and walked out into the lawn followed by Bodie who then flanked off left and crouched ready, he could smell the oncoming danger he knew this was going to be bad and he needed all his strength and wits to be there for his master. Ray took two knives from his belt he held one in each hand and gripped the wooden handles hard until his knuckles turned white. The blades were sharp and of chromed steel, heavy bladed and strong, they would do a lot of damage and Ray had no worry about using them, six inches of steel blade sharpened to a razors edge he had them ready and stood his ground.

Darius looked round and wanted Little John to hurry up and get here, he wished he had called him earlier now, Jan held onto Darius's arm and they watched in fear as the far trees shook, something seemed to of landed there and was barging through towards Ray, who turned and faced whatever was going to come racing at him.

None of them were prepared for what came charging out of the trees, as large as a grizzly bear it had a powerful man like structure a bodybuilders power and look but the head of a wolf, long sharp claws, large sharp pointed teeth, a long white mane that went all the way down its back and ended off into a tail, it was all white that made it look even more menacing under the silver glare of this moon. Its deep red eyes glaring and fixed on Ray, it charged on all fours at first then lifted its self up and ran like a man beast towards him. It's obvious power and strength showed it is stride and toned, hard powerful muscled body, was like an express train coming for him and he was not going to stop it at any price. He didn't have much time to think before the powerful arm swung for his head, as it was in range within seconds. Ray dodged it and lashed out with his knife has he did, the battle had begun. It was no doubt going to be a tumultuous time but this thing was so powerful and so fast and strong it was obvious it was a killing machine and would not back down would not stop and fight until it killed or was killed.

All Ray could do was dodge and counter he had to be fast but he was not going to be fast enough. Jan clasped her hands to her mouth in absolute horror as she watched from the window she had never seen anything so powerful or vicious, it was much stronger than Ray and towered above him, Bodie was circling but couldn't find a target to go for it was all happening too fast and furious.

"What the hell is that thing?" Darius said not taking his worried eyes off the fight on his lawn. The growl and howl of the beast was blood curdling, it caught Ray hard with a gashing blow that cut him open like razors, his arm was bleeding and the jacket he had on was ripped to shreds, Bodie made a dash and clasped his powerful jaws round the leg of the beast but it had no effect, he was stamped on and kicked off, he painfully rolled away with a yelp, he managed to get back to his feet but was much more cautious this time, Ray stabbed and slashed with his blades cutting the beast and spilling its blood but it seemed to have no effect. He circled and moved fast the speed and power of this beast was like nothing he had come across before and that was saying something. He lashed out with his knife at the beasts arms as it swung blows at him, kill its weaponry, so of speak, he thought. Damage what it was using to attack him. But he was caught again and cut down his arm, it was like razor blades slicing his flesh, he backed up but caught another blow to the head, and he staggered back. Bodie made a jump for the beast and locked his teeth round its arm, he shook his head and used his brute strength to try and force the arm down, but was lifted up into the air like he was a piece of meat he was clawed and cut across his belly causing him to let go and awkwardly drop to the ground he was then picked up and hurled away across the garden coming down with a sickening thud that stunned him. Ray dashed in stabbing repeatedly at the beast's throat he managed to get several shots in but was grabbed and pulled towards the opening jaws, the teeth sharper than its claws, he rammed his knife into the mouth and kicked free. He rolled away the knife still stuck in the mouth of this thing; it pulled it out and threw it to the side, blood pouring from its open mouth just made it look even more menacing. It didn't stop it, it just didn't seem to feel pain, it charged forward on all fours at Ray who was scrambling to his feet.

It rammed him viciously knocking him back on to the grass, he rolled and was up on his feet but was seeing double, the adrenalin keeping him going, he dodged down and stabbed into the leg of this creature then rolled off away again, looking back and seeing it seemed to have no effect, how the hell could it be stabbed and ripped open but have no effect? It charged once again and Ray was not quite fast enough it caught him and knocked him off balance he staggered and lost his footing, It pounced and on top of him, again Ray stabbed at the beasts throat with his remaining knife, he was taking blows to the head, his shoulder was gashed open and he cried out in agony. The powerful jaws opened blood pouring out onto his face and were about to come snapping down at his throat. But just at that moment Bodie once again was on the back on the beast ripping into its neck and shoulders. It howled out and turned to grab him, but Bodie, obviously in pain and injured, moved round and bites into the opposite shoulder; Ray could not understand why his knife was not having effect on this thing. His shoulder throbbed and his body was covered in blood his pain screamed at him. He wormed his way out from under the beast trying to get to his feet, as it lifted up to deal with Bodie, as it did he was savagely kicked away and fell to the ground in a heap of agony Angelique was dancing at the end of the garden, she was ecstatic with excitement and joy watching the fight.

Bodie was grabbed and lifted up into the air he was twisting and turning, snapping trying to break free but this beast was just too powerful and strong he felt the grip from the enormous hands tighten round his neck he began to lose breath he could not breathe he struggled more and more but was losing consciousness the beast stood and turning rammed him hard into the ground. Lifted its foot to pound down on Bodies head, but Ray had got to his feet, gathered all the energy and power he had left and rammed the beast while its leg was lifted in the air he managed to knock it off balance and again stabbed furiously at it, his blade going in deep but the power of this thing was never ending and he was hit hard across the head, it dazed him and made him spin round and then the slashing of his back that caused him to stagger and stumble. As the beast came for him it stamped on Bodies body breaking ribs and knocking the dog unconscious. Ray turned but had no strength left he had lost a lot of blood and was dazed he couldn't see anything clearly and just aimlessly hit out. He was picked up and thrown back down like a rag doll; the beast lifted its head and let out a long victorious howl. Ray was moving but only just. He was hurt and hurt bad, it kicked him and he flew across the grass.

Jan dashed into the front room she came back with her automatic in her hand, and a spare magazine down her trousers top, Darius reached out to stop her but she pushed past him and walked out into the garden, she saw Angelique racing forward looking for the kill.

The beast was ramming Ray's limp body down hard into the ground and slashing at his torso ripping him open as it did, the claws digging in and tearing skin and flesh.

Jan took a deep breath and aimed at Angelique, she let off two shots both hitting her in the shoulders she spun back and over on to the grass screaming and wiggling in pain and torment. The two dwellers came to her aid.

The beast snorted out and quickly looked up at Jan it violently pushed the body of Ray to the side, Jan pulled the trigger and stood firm she was a very good shot and all the remaining eighteen bullets hit the beast as it came charging towards her, bit of flesh flew off thudding bullets embedding into the flesh but still it came forward.

She trusted her skill and put faith in her weapon she clipped the magazine out and let it fall she slid the second one in and butted it home with the palm of her hand then pulled the barrel back let it slip and lock into place she took aim and fired, aiming for the head and neck of the beast charging towards her, nerves of steel and her gun hand calm and steady she emptied her remaining magazine in the head and face of the white beast charging like a rhino. The blood showed up more on the white fur and turned it a strong red the face being ripped open and pulverised by the 9mm bullets it slowed and shook it staggered and howled out but it was faltering Jan had only a few bullets left this was the end she was going to be out of ammunition in a matter of seconds. Darius came dashing from the house. Jan pulled the trigger two last times and the two last bullets hit the beast in each eye, exploding those inwards and blowing the back of the head open and out, it screamed and fell sliding in a matted heap of blood and shattered skull bone at her feet only inches away. It breathed out one last agonising breath then was still. The blood seeping into the lawn from its open smashed skull its brains matted and distorted. Blood was pumped out of its arteries then it was silent and still. Destroyed and killed. Jan shook and swallowed she had never been so scared in her life. She caught movement and looked across and she saw Angelique being carried away by the dwellers and then she looked over at Bodie and Ray they both were bleeding and were both still and not moving.

It brought her back to reality and she dashed over to Ray, Darius was already on his way too, they both went to Ray fearing the worse.

"Darius" a voice shouted from the house.

"John thank God you are here, quickly" Darius commanded to Little John who came running to them looking disgusted at the dead beast laying on the lawn a deep patch of blood seeping into the soil under it.

"Jan was talking to Ray to see if he was conscious, she was getting no response, she opened his jacket and shirt, they were covered in blood, she checked his air way was clear, opening his mouth making sure his tongue had not been swallowed. She could see his chest lifting, he was breathing, and he was alive.

"Darius go to my car in the back bring me my black bag, quickly" she ordered has she worked on Ray, Little John went and looked at Bodie he had no idea what had happened but he could easily guess.

"John, go get some towels we need to clean these wounds up, hurry" her voice was urgent and she was trembling but doing her professional best.

"I think the dog is dead", John said has he run past and into the house, Darius ran past him and came to Jan, and he opened her large leather medical bag. She took a small bottle and a syringe, filled some the bottles contents into it then pushed a small amount back out to get rid of air, she pumped all this into Ray, then she searched for something Darius wondered about, it was a tube of super glue, before he said anything she answered him.

"This stuff sticks skin instantly I am using to as a quick fix to seal him up until I stitch the wounds. She worked quickly, and Darius watched impressed at her skill. John came back with some damp towels and they started to clean the blood off his body the best and carefully as they could Jan cut his clothes off with some scissors and shook her head at the gaping wounds he had suffered, she stopped some bleeding, she patched him up she kept checking he was breathing. Taking a small torch she opened Ray's eye and shone this into it checking for brain death. If the pupil constricts, the brain is OK, because in mammals, the brain controls the pupil. She was remembering her collage lecturer giving a talk on it many years ago, why she remembered this she didn't know or care. Darius looked over at the still Bodie of Bodie, he walked over and looked down, the tongue was hanging out of the mouth and the body was still, he knelt down and stroked the matted fur, it was bloody and the wounds on the belly were still bleeding he felt a lump in his throat, then suddenly he saw Bodie twitch, the tongue moved, He was alive.

He dashed from the garden and into the house, he had a good friend who was a vet and had seen Bodie before, he wasted no time in ringing him.

"Lacerations on his back they need stitching I will staple them for now, we need to be careful I have felt for any broken bones but I am not sure of the spinal cord or neck I need a neck brace, I need to get a drip into him" she was more mumbling to herself then to John but he was next to her and did whatever she of asked him.

Eventually she had stopped the bleeding, thanking for mercies that no arteries had been severed, patched his wounds up and now was asking John to find some kind of stretcher they could transport him into the house with. Darius came out and pointed to the garage, they both soon came back with an internal wooden door, Darius had replaced but kept like men do in their garages and garden sheds just in case it might come in handy.

They carefully lifted Ray onto it and being very careful to support his head and neck as they moved him. It was a struggle to get him in the door and then through to the front room, he was placed on the floor, then Jan got to work stitching his wounds together. She was worried about the loss of blood. But her mind was racing she was working under pressure she was trying to remember her training and experience she was fighting back her emotions and she was scared to death of making a mistake, this was the most traumatic night of her life and she just had to stay professional and focused.

Darius had spoke to the vet who was on his way he ran back out to Bodie and pressed a small towel against the belly wound to ease the bleeding. John came out and looked round the area, he had never seen anything like what lay there, a matted blooded shot to pieces animal, larger than a bear with a gaping hole in its head, white fur was stained with blood and it still looked menacing even though it was dead, or at least he hoped it was dead. Gashes in its body and neck where the knives had gone in and tore back out. He walked over to Darius and looked down at Bodie.

"I thought the dog was dead" he said

"I think it almost is, help is on the way, I just hope he gets here in time and can do something when he does, thank you for coming John" Darius looked over to the dead beast.

"What you going to do with that?" John asked

"Burn the bloody thing, burn it back into hell where it came from"

"Ray doesn't look good, Jan looks worried, he is in a right mess, she is stitching him back together and mumbling things to herself, worried there maybe internal injuries or damage to his spinal cord or something, she says she has got to go and get a neck brace but I told her I will get her it and some other things she has at home she needs, will you be alright for half hour if I pop out for her?"

"Yes I will be fine just hurry, get what you need and get back please I am not sure where that bitch Angelique is or planning, quick John be quick"

John hurried away and made double sure what Jan wanted from her home, he took her keys and car and raced off. He was at Jan house in no time the roads were quiet, he rushed in and went to where she had told him to go he picked up the items she wanted and then was racing back in no time. He didn't like the way Ray looked, he had never seen anyone so badly mauled and beat up, the deep cuts were nasty and Jan was doing a good job of getting him back together but what would he be like when or if he awakened. Would he be the same man, it would take so much to come back from this.

The vet didn't like what he saw with Bodie and took him to his surgery he was a good friend of Darius and helped all he could. He was gone by the time John came racing back up the driveway. He ran into the house and gave Jan the items he had brought back she carefully put the neck brace on Ray. She had cleaned the blood off his body and stitched the gaping wounds up, there was a strong smell of antiseptic and he was covered in a blanket to keep him warm, he was battered and bruised swelling over his face and arms his shoulders he looked like he had been run down my a herd of buffalo, and trampled into the ground.

But he was alive and that was the main thing but whether it was a good thing was yet to be seen. Darius came into the room and put his arm around Jan.

"You have done all you can come on sit down you need a drink"

"I don't know, he is not good, I need to get him to a Hospital properly checked out, blood, X-ray ." she shook her head and Darius helped her to sit down.

John went into the garden and with his tremendous strength pulled the beast by its hind leg to the rear of the house, he was going to burn it Like Darius had told him too, and again the night sky should disguise the smoke and stop wondering eyes from investigating.

"You need a stiff drink, don't move" Darius told Jan and went to get her a whisky with a little ice and water, he brought it back and saw she was staring at the still body on the floor of Ray. Giving her the glass she took it and drank half of it down in one gulp. Then laid back on the settee, breathed out and shook her head.

"You have done a great job Jan" Darius said putting his hand compassionately on her shoulder and giving it a slight reassuring squeeze.

"Not sure it is enough he needs better attention then I can give him here, more professional people to help him he needs to be in Hospital maybe I should of not moved him"

"Well we both know that is not possible he can never become a sitting duck in a public place and the questions that will be asked, he lives off the grid, of course you had to move him we have no idea what is out there or was going to happen"

"He will be lucky to live at all Darius, he has lost a lot of blood, if and when he comes round he needs to eat meat, poultry, fish, he will need foods with calcium, B vitamins', Folate, Vitamin C, he could be paralysed because of a broken back or neck this is why you should not move them." She shook her head and finished her drink.

"We will give him whatever he needs and he will awaken you will see"

Laying back Jan took a deep breath and closed her eyes, Darius took the glass of her and let her rest. He went outside and picked the automatic up off the lawn where Jan had dropped it going to see to Ray, he brought this back into the house then walked round to where John was preparing the fire to burn this beast from hell. He had poured petrol over the body and encased it in some wood he found in the garage. He lit a piece of rolled up newspaper and stood back he then threw it onto the beast, the petrol ignited instantly and engulfed the white fur and body, it soon caught fire the body fat burning and the wood keeping it going, the flames danced high and turned a orange colour, they both stood back and looked at the unusual way the flames were dancing high into the sky, suddenly they began to look round at each other. The body of the beast moved, it rolled and it went into spasm, could it not be dead? Darius backed up and John came by his side, the flames turned blood red, and got higher and higher into the night sky. It was a beautiful but somehow disturbing sight, the body of the beast rose up off the ground the fire blazing around and over it, the fur all gone the flesh dripping off its bones. The roar of the fire fell silent, no noise just the flames the body suspended in mid air burning away getting less and less, the body was soon gone and a grotesque skeleton shape was left. The flames turned yellow then orange then they seem to disappear but in fact they were jet black, the bones began to powered and drift away up into the sky with the black flames, which slowly turned to a deep red once again, Soon there was nothing left, the flames of the fire had taken and claimed the whole body back, there was nothing left except some burning wood, the moon shone bright and a distant howl could just be heard, it sent a shiver down their spines. They backed away and looked around them. It was silent and still, Then the crack of the fire was there and the wood burning away, there was no trace what so ever of the beast, none.

They both came back into the house and John went round making sure all the windows and doors were locked and they were secured in for the evening.

None of them slept much that night and just kept each other company, what had happened was such a terrible thing it only hit them while they were calming and seeing the battered tortured body of the warrior Ray on the floor in front of them.

Jan kept going to him and checking, he was stable as possible, he was out cold and she just hoped he would come round and able to talk and move and walk again.

The sun slowly rose in the sky and the night was pushed away, the light showed up the deep blood stain on the lawn the battlefield, the grass had been ripped up and there was muddy patched where the fight had raged. Darius went and picked up the empty shells from the grass which flew out of Jan's gun when she fired it the night before. He disposed of these and went back into the house, John was making everyone eggs and bacon and Jan was looking at the dressings on Ray's body.

The phone rang and Darius answered it, he nodded and grunted a few answers then put the phone back down he walked into the Kitchen.

"The dog, Bodie, is in a bad way, has been operated on, he had busted ribs and internal bleeding he has a fifty, fifty chance of surviving" he sat down and drank some coffee that was ready for him. Jan came in and sat next to him.

John dished out the breakfast, and they all ate in silence, alone with their own thoughts.

The screams could not be heard because she was underground and in darkness, the dwellers had got her back but it took the all night to do so, she had passed out and they had to carry her, they could see perfectly well it the dark and in their lair under the forest. Angelique could not she had no idea what was happening and she had become delirious, the bullets were still lodged in her shoulders and they had to come out, it was going to be a painful operation. She was screaming in pain, but also in anguish at not seeing what had happened to Ray she had no idea if he was alive or dead and it destroyed her, the dwellers went to work holding her down and digging the two bullets out of her flesh, she tried to twist and turn but she was held firmly down awhile the bullets were painfully and dangerously dug out, there was no compassion no thought of sympathy they just did what had to be done, she screamed and then passed out once again with the pain, they welcomed it and carried on doing what they had to do, eventually they were able to get the bullets out and they packed the wounds with a mixture of their own spit and mashed up berries one of them got from the forest, they pushed it into the hole and then made sure she didn't move, some of them stayed with her the others moved off and way into the tunnels and were gone out of sight.

The day became bright and sun got high, it would have been a beautiful day except for the circumstances on both sides. Jan again checked on Ray, he was still unconscious but this gave his body time to heal its self the mind needed all its power and ability to fix its broken parts and stop him from the trauma of the pain.

"How is he, still out cold?" John asked coming into the room.

"Yes, he is, hope he doesn't slip into a coma, just hope he is not paralysed just hope.." She stopped and shook her head holding back her tears; John came over and put his large and strong arm round her .she fell into him and welcomed the comfort.

"He will make it, he is a strong bastard, he will get through this you will see, and nothing is going to hold him down for long,

"I hope not John, I hope not"

"Darius said you were amazing last night you saved everyone with your shooting skill"

"Who was it who said never send a man where you can send a bullet?"

"I have no idea but it is a bloody good saying"

Jan smiled and pulled away she looked down at Ray then walked to the stairs, she smiled at John and went up for a shower. She stayed in there for some time washing the night before from her body the smell, the fear, the memory, but she knew it would never go away, she just hoped she had done enough and he would recover.

Darius visited his friend who had Bodie, he wanted to thank him properly for doing all he had done and continued to do. Bodie was out cold also he had bandages round his mid section and was on a drip some of his fur had been shaved away he looked in a weak state and not very well. He had taken a battering also and needed the attention of people who cared and wanted the best for him.

He bought some supplies and went back to the house in the afternoon, John was still up and keeping an eye about the place, Jan was asleep up stairs she was shattered and exhausted.

"How is the dog?" John asked sitting down at the kitchen table.

"Looks like Ray at the moment they have had to operate on him, and he had fractured ribs, he is all bandaged up and out cold" he came and sat across from John.

"So what happens now, how do we know there is not more of them bloody things on the way, what about this woman you were talking about, where is she?"

"I have no idea, I know Jan shot at her but I have no idea what happened to her, I am hoping she is dead, vile bloody woman, the main concern now is to keep them safe until they are back on their feet again" Darius looked at John with doubt in his eyes.

"Do you think that will happen, Jan is scared he is going to be brain dead or something, a coma she talked about?"

"Well let's stay positive and hope for the best we will not know until he comes round will we, no use trying to cross bridges we have not come to yet"

"You want me to stick around for a while, might be more trouble coming?"

"Yes if you will John, thank you so much for your help, again, you are a good and true friend" Darius stood up and went to put the shopping away he had got.

"I owe you much, you helped me when no one else did, I thank you my good friend"

The rest of the day went by uneventfully, Jan got up late afternoon after a few hours sleep, then John got his head down for a while he was planning on staying on guard all night so needed some rest. Darius made them food in the evening and there was not much else they could do, Jan constantly checked on Ray and was pleased he was sustaining himself with breathing, he just seemed to be asleep and resting she kept him warm with blankets and kept checking for the signs of broken bones, the swelling was coming out and his face was puffed up the skin turning bruised then yellow. The night was a quieter one and they all seemed to calm somewhat, again the sun broke the darkness and John wet to bed he had stayed up all night keeping a diligent watch. Jan was at in the living room and looking at Ray then her eyes widened, was that movement? She was not sure, his mouth twitched she was sure of it, she dashed towards him and knelt down, she said his name, touching his head she stroked his hair. Be there was no response. She sighed and looked up at Darius who had come into the room from the kitchen.

"Anything?" he asked

"I thought so, but no, nothing, at least he is breathing by himself that is a good sign"
She stood up and walked back to her chair, Darius turned to go back into the kitchen, then they both spun round and stared down at Ray.

He growled and his mouth opened, he took a deep breath and then let out a sigh, Darius dashed forward tripping over Jan as she got in his way springing up from the chair they both fell to the floor and knelt holding each other by Ray's side, looking at him for more signs. His eyes flickered open and he cursed out, swallowing, he licked his lips and blinked several times. His took deep breaths, and turned his head slightly.

Jan held her hand to her mouth she had tears in her eyes, Darius leaned forward saying.
"How do you feel Ray?"

"Stupid question don't you think, How the hell do I look?" was Ray's answer
"Jan watched and her joy turned to a frown, she reached out and held Rays hand but got no response, she then squeezed his finger and still got no response. The joy was suddenly turning sour; she moved her hand down his legs and to his toes.

"Why the hell can I not move?" Ray rocked his head and was confused.

"Ray can you feel my hand on your foot, can you feel my pressing on your toes?" Jan asked
"What? Why the bloody hell, can I not move?" he became agitated and his breathing became erratic. Jan put her hand on his head and stroked his forehead. She looked at Darius with dread and sadness in her eyes.

Darius could see something was desperately wrong and Jan knew what it was, she held back her tears and just tried to calm Ray she gathered her strength and made sure her voice did not falter or show her fear.

"You have had a very traumatic experience, your body has shut its self down, it's like a safety mechanism, you will get feeling back soon, don't worry Ray just rest and keep strong"

"I can't bloody move, why can I not move?" his voice was louder and filled with anger, the pain from his head started to make its self felt the thumping of the concussion the battering he had taken, but he had no feeling from the neck down.

Jan tried to calm him but he was confused and angry and getting more confused, Darius took his hand but then realised what a stupid thing it was to do because he could not feel anything, he let it go again and just looked down at him.

"Ray, Ray stay calm you need to stay calm you are going to fix, it will just take some time" Jan tried to convince him but fighting back her real fears was not easy.

"Bodie, where is Bodie? I want him with me" Ray shouted angrily

"Bodie is fine he just needed some attention he is alive and well at the vets I was with him yesterday. " Darius reassured him. Albeit a white lie thrown in.

"Listen, Listen to me, you have had a severe head injury and severe trauma, it is temporary paralysis you are experiencing that is all, now stop getting angry you are doing yourself no good you have to stay calm you have some nasty injuries and lost a lot of blood" Jan was trying her best to calm the situation and held her emotions back the best she could she had to be professional for all their sakes.

"How do you know its temporary?" Ray asked calm all of a sudden and serious, looking at her with his piercing blue eyes and swollen face.

"Because nothing keeps a man like you down now shhhh and rest"

"I have a bad taste in my mouth, what is this thing round my neck?"

Darius got up to get him a drink, he found a straw and filled a glass full of milk bringing it back he could see Jan had calmed him down somewhat, Ray drank the milk and said no more.

He rested and was quiet, he was alone now with his thoughts and Jan left him comfortable, she walked into the kitchen and Darius hugged her as she sobbed quietly into his shoulder.

"I should have not moved him, I should have called an ambulance straight away" she said quietly through her tears.

"You did what you had to do, there was no time Jan, you had no choice" his words were comforting and heartfelt but there was dismay in his voice.

Ray said no more he was quiet and seemed in deep thought, John stayed up all night but they didn't talk, Ray seemed far away and almost in a trance like state. John kept guard and made sure everything was secure. He was sat in a chair when the sun finally came up. Ray had dropped off to sleep in the early hours of the morning; they had not spoken although Ray had been awake all night. John didn't impose and left him be, he knew he was there and would ask if he needed anything.

Jan was down first she looked tired and worried, she had saddened eyes and glanced over at Ray as she walked into the kitchen, John got up and went into the kitchen to see if she was alright, he could see she wasn't.

"Anything I can do for you Jan?" he asked solemnly

"No, thank you I will be ok, was there any trouble through the night?" she nodded over to where Ray was.

"No, he didn't make a sound or move." he grimaced at his last remark.

Jan leaned back on the work surface tears in her eyes, she shook her head and John came to comfort her, she looked up at him tears rolling down her face, he didn't know what to do, hug her, or let her come to him, he stood there confused.

It was an awkward moment but Jan smiled bravely through her tears, touched his shoulder and walked into the room to where Ray lay. She dried her eyes and took a deep breath, she had been thinking a lot throughout the night and had to be straight with Ray, she felt it only right, she would want to be told if it was her in this position and thought Ray would also. She sat on the chair and looked down at him, his eyes were closed and he looked peaceful. She sat there and just looked at him for a while then was startled when he spoke but didn't open his eyes.

"What you looking at?" he said but she wasn't sure if it was in a humours way or not.

"Oh you are awake?" she said smiling but he still didn't open his eyes.

"I am always awake except when I am having nightmares" he opened his eyes slowly and tilted his head to look at her. His gaze cut through her and she could feel the cold and calculated stare of a warrior, a man who would do anything to survive, none of the Ray she had known a few days earlier, this was a different man altogether.

"I hope you didn't have any nightmares last night"

"Jan let's cut the crap, I want you to promise me something, and it is in your capability to do it for me, will you follow through if need be?"

"What do you mean, I don't understand, I will do anything I can for you"

"Remember you have said them words, If I am like this forever, kill me, you can do it Jan inject me or whatever but do not leave me like this, I do not want to live like this, never want to be left in this state." He was serious and cold and his eyes were dark without sentiment or emotion." He stared her in the eye and she felt cold with a shiver running down her spine.

"Ray, I have a friend who runs a private clinic. We are getting you there and x-rayed, to see what the problems are, you will be safe there is it not a hospital and no one will know you are there, please just don't give up on us"

"What happened to the temporally paralysis you spoke of yesterday? Why were you crying in the kitchen to Darius, do not treat me like a fucking child, if this is it, tell me, kill me now"

"NO, no Ray stop talking like that, we just need time that is all"

"Where is Bodie, I want him with me"

"He is at the vets, they had to operate and pin some of his ribs back together he is stable so don't worry about him, he will be ok, the lungs were not damaged he just needs rest too"

"I want him here with me"

"I don't know if he can be moved, we need to get you to the clinic I am ringing about it today" Jan was trying to stay professional but finding it very hard indeed.

"Fuck the Clinic, I want Bodie and I want the truth, the truth Jan" his voice had raised and his face had become agitated with frustration, and fear his breathing was becoming irregular. She knelt by his side and put her hand on his forehead, looking into his eyes she decided there and then to tell him what she thought.

"Listen to me very carefully, a severe head injury can cause brain damage, the brains surface can tear or bruise, this damages blood vessels and nerves, Paralysis can occur if a part of the brain that controls specific muscles is damaged during a severe head injury. Damage to the left side of the brain can cause paralysis to the right side of the body and damage to the right side can cause the same to the left side of the body"

"I can't move either fucking side, what does that mean?" Ray asked seeming more calm and less frustrated.

"The spinal cord might be damaged, which mean the nerves which carry the signals to your body from the brain may no longer be getting through. Able to transmit the signal so causing paralysis, the higher up the damage the more worse the paralysis will be, for example, an injury in the middle of the spine will usually cause what we call Paraplegia, which is paralysis of the lower limbs, a neck injury, such as a broken neck will usually result in what we call quadriplegia, paralysis in all four limbs, as well as normal lung function, which means you might need a ventilator to breath, but you can breathe perfectly well so that is a good sign" she tried to sound uplifting more for herself then for him she felt.

Ray looked at her and for a moment said nothing he pierced into her eyes and she felt uncomfortable but retuned his stare for a short time until she had to look away.

"I am paralysed from the neck down, there is no way I am going to live like this, I want you to bring me Bodie, and I want you to bring me my Ouija board and place it on my chest, I want you to stop getting upset and thinking you have done anything wrong" his voice was surprisingly calm now, she was crying and looked back at him.

"There is a chance it is temporary, trauma can bring it on, we need to run some tests I am getting in touch with my friend today, there is lots that can be done, treatments, that can be administered, maybe exercises that will stimulate..." Ray shook his head at her and she stopped talking.

"Do as I ask, and stop beating yourself up about things, and what happened to that fucking bitch?"

"I hit her with two bullets and we have no idea where she is" Jan had resumed some calm herself and looked back at him.

"She will be back, if she can muster demons like that fucking thing she will be back, she is weak by herself but can summon things to do her dirty work, that is what was puzzling about her, she was not powerful enough to do much herself but could muster up help"

"We need to get you safe Ray"

"I am not and cannot go anywhere; if it is to end then it is now and here, take this bloody thing off my neck" he moved his head round and without thinking she just bent down and took the neck brace off him. Darius came into the room he had been listening from the bottom of the stairs; John was stood next to him.

"I have been telling Ray what the situation is" Jan said looking at them both.

Ray moved his eyes to look at them all stood to his side and looking down at him, he looked at each one individually then at them all as a group.

"OK, no more tears no more feeling sorry about anything, if it is going to happen it is going to happen, I want Bodie here and my Ouija, that is all I ask, can you please do that now for me" he didn't wait for an answer he looked away again and sighed out.

No one said anything and Darius went out to his friends the vets to see if Bodie could be moved, John walked back into the kitchen and looked out of the window, he was tired and needed some sleep. Jan walked up to him and hugged him, he put his arm round her and she stayed there for a moment, just to be held it felt good and she needed a hug right now.

"You look tired John go get some rest" she said finally pulling away from him, he nodded and asked in a friendly and concerned voice.

"Are you sure you are going to be alright Jan?"

"Yes we will be fine, don't worry, if I need you I know where you are my good friend"

John went up stairs and Jan came back to sit with Ray, she knelt down and checked his dressings to see if they needed changing. He said nothing and just watched her for a short time. She was thinking that Ray may never walk or be able to move again, it was a horrid thought to have about anyone but somehow it seemed a thousand times worse because it was him. She tried to dismiss it from her mind.

"Stop over thinking and worrying Jan" Ray said serenely.

"I am sorry, so sorry, I should not of moved you your spinal cord may of been damaged and it could be my fault, how do I live with that Ray?" she turned to him for an answer tears again dwelling in her eyes.

"You did nothing wrong, if it is it is, nothing can be done about it now, but remember my words here and now, listen to me,, it is not your fault do you understand, none of this is your fault, it is mine, I was not fast or good enough, it was bound to happen sooner or later, so stop all this self blame and pity. I will take you over my knee and spank your arse if there is any more of it, so let's stop it and go make me a cup of tea and see if we have any biscuits"

She stood up hiding her tears once more and went into the kitchen to make a mug of tea for him. She came in while the kettle was boiling, with a small mirror and placed it in the window sill then came round and past Ray who asked her.

"What the hell is that?"

"It is a charged mirror, for protection"

"A mirror?" what the bloody hell is that going to do.

" A charged mirror to protect, white magic is powered by love and you have a lot of people who love you Ray, although we want peace and no harm to come to any animal the black art witchcraft does many vile things and you take them away, there are some who do not agree with what you do but there and many who do agree, and that many will do all they can to protect you as they always do, spells are always being cast in your favour, and many will be cast now for you to get well, it is a very powerful force"

"Yeah I am sure, thank you"

She made him tea and fed him biscuits and they chatted, she actually chatted with this warrior who was now incapable of feeding himself, but she didn't mind one bit, she appreciated what he had said to her about not blaming herself, it had meant a lot. He had made her feel at ease and was totally unselfish about his situation, he seemed calm and has accepted it all of a sudden, it was strange to Jan but nothing really surprised her anymore about this man.

It was some hours later when Darius came back he slowly walked Bodie in, who was very tentative he slowly walked and looked weak, he came up to Ray and his tail wagged, he had shaven fur where the operation had taken place the stitches were visible and he was obviously in a lot of discomfort licking Rays face he let out a little yelp has he got lay down.

"He needs to be still, he is on pain killers, and very weak, he need lots of rest and the less movement the better" Darius said, has he watched Bodie painfully lay next to Ray and they both looked at each other. Jan could see it would be very therapeutic for them both to be together; she went to Ray's car and brought him his Ouija board, placing it on his chest as he had asked.

She changed some of the dressings and fed Ray his food that evening and the night closed in again John stayed up and watched over them all keeping guard. It was again an uneventful night something none of them complained about. Darius had a long talk with Ray and they seemed to be discussing older times, Ray spoke and chatted quite readily and it puzzled them somewhat why he was not worried at all. Or maybe he was just very good at covering it up. The Ouija board stayed with him at his own request, Bodie was quiet and rested and never left his side, it all seemed so quiet, so safe, but they knew at any moment at any second it could be shattered and if anything now came for Ray he wouldn't not stand a chance, but Jan and her sisters all were helping with their spells, there emanating power of love and healing, Ray was sceptical of the charged mirror but Jan knew it was a powerful tool to ward off evil. That night Ray had a restless time, John told Darius he was talking a lot in his sleep, he was sweating and kept waking up. The next day Ray looked tired, he didn't speak much and just seemed away with his thoughts, Bodie never left his side and they both settled down mid afternoon. The house was quiet and Jan went home for a while to get some things she needed, and sort some things out. She had no idea how long she would have to be here but she didn't mind, she headed back quickly. Darius went about his business and it all just seems so tranquil and safe, but they all knew it wasn't. Deep down they were all scared and worried but tried to stay strong for each other and especially for Ray.

CHAPTER SIX

The howling was distant but Bodie heard it, Rays eyes flickered open, he looked round and Bodie was up on his feet growling at the door. The room was dark and the house quiet, the howling from the beast got louder, the laugh of Angelique was hackling from outside. Ray looked round the room, it was too quiet, he couldn't move, he cursed and felt helpless. Bodie was unsteady on his feet, in pain and growling, his hair raised on his back. "Darius, John" Ray shouted out, but no one appeared.

Ray gritted his teeth he was totally helpless, the only thing that could now save him was Bodie, who himself was damaged and in pain. The howling roared outside and it seemed to shake the houses very foundations, Ray turned and saw Jan running down the stairs with her gun ready she looked at the door just as it was ripped off its hinges and pulled out into the garden, moments later the large beast from before was there, the huge bulk filling the doorway it howled and kicked Bodie across the room has he ran forward, Jan took aim but was to late it was in front of her within less than a second it swung a wide blow and almost severed her head from her shoulders. Ray cried out in anger and frustration, it grabbed the body of Jan and then ripped her head completely off, throwing the torso aside and the head to follow, Ray was grabbed by the hair and dragged across the floor and out into the garden he was flung across the lawn and rolled onto his side. He looked up at the beast bearing down at him snarling and growling at him, Angelique was walking across the grass laughing, she looked at her right hand she was dragging something across the grass behind her, he peered and as she came closer and nearer to the light from the house he could see it was the corpse of Christine, being dragged by the hair behind her. She let out a malevolent laugh and threw the corpse next to him, he looked at the decaying body of his once love, it was not a pretty sight and he diverted his eyes, Bodie stagger to the door way and tried to run but just could not. This was it, Ray was about to die, this was going to be the end, he was not even going to die fighting, not on his feet, but helpless and unable to retaliate he closed his eyes and cursed out loud. Darius came running out of the house with John, Ray shouted to them to run, to save themselves and get away but they didn't seem to hear him, they both dashed forward to try and help but the beast was to powerful and quick it ripped Darius with its sharp large claws across the stomach he fell clutching his mid section and dropped to his knees in agonising pain losing blood through his fingers as he tried to close the gaping wound. John turned and picked up a large branch he was going to use as a weapon but again he was not fast enough, he swung the branch at the beast but it had no effect, he was lifted up in the air above the head and brought smashing down onto the beasts bent knee snapping his back in two and killing him out right with the sheer force and power of it.

Angelique screamed with feverish laughter, she danced round and swung her arms about like a demented child.

She came to Ray and kicked him savagely in the head reeling it back and breaking his nose, blood poured out and he had to shake his head and spit out the blood from his mouth. She flung out her arm and where she pointed an inferno of flames suddenly appeared. A roaring fire like a he had never seen fiercely danced only yards from him. The body of John was picked up and thrown into the flames then the beast lifted Darius up with one arm, Darius screamed and looked at Ray who could do nothing to help. He was tossed into the fire still alive and his screams pierced Ray's ears, he closed his eyes and cursed out loud spitting abuse at Angelique. She dashed into the house and brought out the headless corpse of Jan she threw this into the flames also and laughed and danced about with sheer joy of it.

Bodie was struggling to run he walked and barked and bravely came to Ray's side standing over his body.

"Run Bodie, go, go lad now" Ray pleaded more than commanded.

Bodie stood solid he was not going to leave his master, the beast stood looking at them waiting for the command, Angelique walked calmly toward them and looked Ray in the eye.

"Not so much a warrior now, more of a pathetic helpless useless piece of crap to be tossed aside and burned in hell for all eternity"

"Bodie, go" was all Ray could say.

The corpse of Christine was lifted up by Angelique and tossed into the fire also, she laughed at the flames devouring the flesh, and all that was left now was Ray and Bodie. She turned and stared at them both, Ray knew Bodie would die before he left Rays side. Ray was in absolute torture, not physically but mentally, there was nothing he could do, this was the end of it all and this is what he had come too, a helpless and hopeless mess.

The beast came forward and stamped onto Bodie who was unable to stop him he yelped out as his ribs were crushed into his lungs and he was held there by the weight and power of the beast, Angelique dragged Ray and carefully with tremendous strength threw his body into the flames but only his body so he could see himself burn, his head was left outside of the inferno he had no feeling so he would just watch himself burn until he was no more.

Suddenly Ray sensed something, it was strange but so powerful so strong, he had no idea what it was no time to think but he knew something was there something prevailing and it confused him. He looked into the flames he saw hands reaching up clawing at him trying to pull him down, he saw hideous faces snarling at him, he saw faces from things he had killed before faces or witches, demons, all the things he had sent to hell were now wanting to pull him down with them. He felt the heat on his face, his body melting in the flames, he turned and looked at Bodie, the beast had him held out in front of it. Suddenly without warning the beast ripped Bodie in two, that is what tipped Ray over the edge and he cried out with anguish with pain with regret and with so much force, the second before he saw a face, it was the face of a woman, she looked Hispanic she was beautiful she had long black hair, she was looking into his eyes, she was holding out her arms.

"Bodie" Ray screamed out for the last time while the flames engulfed him and he was dragged down into hell.

He rolled over the floor sweat pouring down his face, he staggered up to his feet then fell onto the floor again in agony, his whole body ached and retched him with pain, he was confused and dazed he didn't know where he was, he looked round seeing Jan looking at him, Darius and John coming towards him, he was in the house, he was alive he looked for Bodie, he was there looking back at him, Ray shook his head, he didn't know what was happening.

"Ray, fuck sake Ray, you moved, you are moving" Jan said crying through her hand she had up against her mouth, she could not believe it, he was moving he was no longer paralysed?

He was breathing heavily; he was totally confused for a moment but then took deep breaths, had it been a nightmare? He looked round again, Bodie painfully walked towards him, Ray put his hand round Bodies neck, he was in pain, but he didn't care he was with his dog again and they were both alive he rested his head on Bodies.

Jan had stopped Darius and John they all just looked on in total amazement at this miracle happening before them. They gave him a few moments, to regain composure, to get his bearings, to try and understand what the hell had happened. Jan shook her head, how could this be? Ray was on his knees, the aching and stiffness in his body made itself, known, the bandages were showing blood where he had burst stitches, but Jan knew she could fix that, she was in total disbelief in what she was seeing.

Darius walked to Ray and knelt down by his side. He put his hand on his shoulder.

"Ray, are you alright" he asked quietly

"I have no bloody idea, to be honest, but I need to sort this mess out and get on with it" Ray let Bodie go lay back down, he looked up at Jan.

"It is impossible what you are doing?" she told him.

"I had a terrifying dream, I was burning in hell fire, Bodie...", he shook his head and didn't want to think about it, Ray sat back and felt the pain driving through his entire body.

"How do you feel? Can you move your toes, can you feel your fingers?" Jan was shaking her head and had no idea what was going on.

"Jan I feel like I have been hit by an express train, I ache all over and yes I can feel everything, what the hell is happening you said I was paralysed?"

"I have no idea, never seen or heard of anything like it" she looked round and saw the Ouija laying by the side of where Ray had been moments earlier, she looked at John who was stood waiting to be told what to do, and Darius next to Ray who turned and said.

"If it was trauma that brought the paralysis on, then maybe trauma took it away again, like you hear of someone being blind all their life then get a knock on the head and they can see suddenly, no one can explain why, or how the Buddhist monks seem to heal themselves or how suddenly someone gets a tremendous amount of strength when in a certain situation they lift cars off their loved one who are trapped, you read about stories like this, maybe it was brought on with the trauma of what happened Rays mind shut down his body for some reason, now this nightmare has triggered it back?" Darius was half asking, half guessing. Jan shook her head, but she had no medical explanation or a better one so just accepted what Darius said, it made it all much easier.

"Your dressings need changing Ray, looks like you have opened a wound on your shoulder, let me fix it" Jan got up and went for her medical bag.

Darius stood up and looked at Bodie who was not taking his eyes off Ray from where he lay next to him on the floor.

"Tea, I want some tea and have you any biscuits left?" Ray said matter of factly that made every one nervously laugh, which was a good way to relive their stress and confusion. John went into the kitchen and made the tea, while Jan saw to Rays wounds, she patched him up and cleaned where he had stretched the stitches in his skin, she said nothing, but was holding back tears as she tended to the wounds on his battered body, the bruising, the swelling, he really did look like he had been hit by a train, several times.

Ray stretched his fingers out, he moved his neck in a circular motion, he was stiff and achy but at least he could move, he was just as confused as everyone else, but he was more relived as well. Stretching a leg out, he groaned in pain and gritted his teeth.

"Be still a moment while I do this please" Jan said sternly.

"I need to get moving, need to sort that bitch out, find her kill her and get moving"

"You are not going anywhere for a while, you will need time to heal and it will not happen overnight, so stay still and shut up and let me do this please" she said changing some of his dressings and cleaning up the wounds. He did has he was told, he looked over at Bodie who was looking back at him, then he looked Jan in the eyes as she tended to his wounds, he watched her and she tried to ignore his gaze she knew he was looking at her.

John brought in the tea, and a packet of biscuits, he placed them down by Ray and one next to Jan and backed up looking at Darius who had walked into the room.

"We are going to lock up for the night have we got everything we need, it is getting dark?" Darius said not waiting for an answer as him and John went and secured the house. Jan finished up and stood up taking the used bandages with her, Ray stood; he was unsteady and had to stretch a little to make his aching body move.

"Sit down, you need to rest" Jan ordered as she came back into the room.

"I need a piss that is what I need" Ray said bluntly he struggled up stairs and went into the bath room, he washed and watered and got himself some clothes to wear, he found it hard and difficult to move but was not going to give up and was determined not to be beat. He came back down the stairs and slowly and painfully sat in a chair. He eased down and breathed out has he did, he stretched out his legs and circled his foot one at a time, Jan watched and shook her head in disbelief she had no explanation for what she was seeing.

Ray cursed when he noticed he had left his tea and biscuits on the floor, but before he got up, Jan had stood and got them for him, she handed them to him and sat back down across the room on the settee.

Ray opened the biscuits and dipped two into his tea then ate them, Jan smiled to herself, it was like having him back and she was very pleased about it.

"So how are you feeling apart from stiff sore and being hit by a train" Jan asked

"I will be ok now, just needed to get on my feet; I will heal up and get going"

"I don't know the hell you manage it Ray, your body must be made from steel, to bounce back after what you go through is amazing"

"Like I said Jan, I have no choice, I give up I am dead, it is a strong incentive tha knows lass?" he said in thick Yorkshire accent.

"It is nothing short of a miracle that is what it is"

Ray closed his eyes, the pain in his head was beginning to thump harder and he sighed out, Jan knew what was wrong and went to get him some pain killers, she handed them to him and he took them without question.

"Thank you, for all you have done for me Jan, you are an amazing woman" he said resting his head back and closing his eyes. Within a few minutes he was asleep again. Jan stood up and took the mug of tea out of his hand and let him rest, it was the best thing for him.

That night everyone slept more content, Darius stood guard and gave John a break, nothing happened. Bodie was a little restless but that was down to his injuries more than anything else, the sun came up on a more content household.

That morning Jan was cleaning her gun, Darius was making breakfast and John and Ray were still sleeping, a slight knock came to the back door, Jan looked up startled and then across at Bodie who was also sleeping and had not moved which she found extremely strange, she loaded her weapon and walked into the kitchen Darius was looking out of the window and trying to see who it was. He walked to the door and slowly opened it.

Standing there was a beautiful woman, Hispanic looking with black hair down just past her shoulders, she had a high forehead her eyes were dark but welcoming, she had smouldering good looks and dressed very well and tidy, she smiled at Darius and then looked at Jan holding her gun out pointing it at her. Lifting her hands in an open manner she said in a very polite voice.

"I assure you that will not be needing that, I have come in peace and want to help, and believe me, my help is needed, may I come in for a moment?"

"You can say what you have to say from there, who are you?" Jan said frowning The woman smiled and sighed slightly then looked up and started talking in a voice that spoke of good up bringing and intelligence, she confidant and stood straight and proud.

"My name is Sophia, and I am here to help, to help your Warrior because he is in need of it more now than ever"

"You some sort of witch?" Darius said confused

"No, I am not a witch, I am a follower and a guardian of good and fighter of evil, I have known of Ray for many years, I have been watching, following, always there but he would not have noticed me, I can track him much like Lillian does through his Ouija, he now needs help and I can give it to him. Many of you pray for him, cast spells in his favour, but I am one of the few whom actually protect the warrior Ray, we have power to help him and have done in the past, I was never going to make myself felt or seen, but he has never been so vulnerable as he is now, the paralysis will pass but he needs much time to heal, time he doesn't really have. Christine was taken and tricked she was destroyed and we have to make sure Angelique doesn't do the same to him, she will not stop until she succeeds or is destroyed trying."

"How can we trust you, how come we have never known about you before, I have never heard of you." Jan said with scepticism

"I was not needed before like I am now, let Ray decide, let him touch me and feel the vibe he needs to feel, let Bodie scent me and see there is no evil against them. Let them decide, let them choose, if they do not want me to help I will leave, but I will bid the warrior farewell because without my help he is a dead man"

Jan pointed her gun at this woman and looked at her in the eye; they stared at each other for a moment, trying to work each other out.

"It is strange you should come now, why have you not made yourself known earlier, who are you? How do you know so much? It is very odd and suspicious" Darius said.

"I am a guardian of the good, Darius, I know it must seem very suspicious to you and I do not blame you, but I am here to help and Ray will confirm that once he touches me he will know"

"No, we don't need your help so just bugger off where it is you came from" Jan said

"Let her in" Ray said from the front room door way where he was stood and watching them, Jan turned and shook her head.

"No, Ray we don't know who the hell she is, she knows too much"

"I saw you in my dream, you were there" Ray said walking past Jan and Darius to stand in front of this woman.

"Yes I pulled you back, it is a bad and dangerous time for you, and you need all the help you can get" she smiled and it lit up her face and she seemed to beam beauty out to him. Jan felt jealous and Darius was confused, but Ray seemed content she was safe.

He invited her in and they went to the front room and sat down. They chatted and Ray listened intensely to what she was saying, Jan stayed in the kitchen with Darius and looked dejected somewhat.

"Don't worry Jan; she must be safe, Ray would of known otherwise"

"I don't like it, who the hell is she? Who does she think she is just strolling in here, and how the fuck did she know he was here anyway?"

Darius could sense a hit on jealousy and decided to leave it, Jan was trying to listen to what was being said, but have enough respect to give Ray the privacy he obviously wanted.

"So you see Ray I have been on your side for many years, I do not know how this was bestowed upon me but I have it, and can see and protect you through it" Sophia was trying to explain to him as simply as possible.

"I have never seen you but always felt something there, sometimes I wondered if there was other forces at hand, the luck I had, the times I should have been caught but never was, I know Lillian makes herself felt but I get a very strange and unique vibe from you something I have not had from anyone else"

"I am very pleased to hear that, I am honoured to hear that actually, I am sorry about Christine and what happened"

"Thank you, but I can't do anything about that now, it is something I will have to live with and I will have to deal with what is at hand more importantly"

"Yes of course, she must be destroyed and you must do it soon, she can summon from hell, so be careful, but you must concentrate on getting fit and well, you have taken one hell of a battering, and you are going to need all your strength"

"How did you get into my nightmare? How did you pull me out and through this?"

"I have been in touch with the other side all my life, I knew when things were going to happen before they happened, I could see into people's souls, I know a good man or a bad man as soon as I look at them. when I got older I was more and more seeing this man who was battling evil, he was a warrior and had such a magnificent lineage going back to medieval times, I use to dream of his adventures then come to realise they were not really dreams they were me seeing what was actually happening"

"All your life, you cannot be that old"

"I am forty three"

"No bloody way you look in your late twenties" Ray was genuinely taken back with surprised

"Well thank you kind sir, she smiled at him and he liked the look very much. I got to see you in action, were somehow in touch with you in some way but I could not understand why or how, then I used an Ouija board and it was very strange the thing just kept flying away from me as if it didn't want me to use it. One day I was contacted by Lillian she knew what was happening she enlightened me and showed me what I must to, I learned to control the dreams to inter react, if you like, this way I was able to help you. I was a guardian of the good, a protector and an adversary of evil, of the darkness"

"Lillian always said there are ones who were helping me; I see what she means now"

"Yes I would help when I was in dream mode if you like, it has been like this for a long time, I often felt what you felt and knew what you were doing, not all good, but you are doing something no one else can or has ever done, I always have helped you, when I saw you in the state you were in this time I knew it would be the end if I didn't do something I came into your dream I broke into your subconscious if you like, it was not easy I had to live your nightmare feel every bit of it, then give you everything I had to pull you out of it, but not only pull you back but to fix you to make you move again. Your body was not broken it was your mind, you needed to bring your mind and heart back together this is when you can walk again, I did my best to get you back and just hope I did enough" she bowed her head .

Ray lifted her chin with his hand and looked into her dark smouldering eyes, he smiled.

"You did one hell of a job and I will be forever in your debt, if there is anything I can ever do to repay you, never hesitate to ask me"

She smiled and stared deep into his blue eyes she searched his soul and delved into his heart, he sensed it and did nothing to stop it, for once in his life he actually welcomed someone looking deep within him, she made him feel so different, she looked to his very soul and she was not disappointed with what she found. Sohpia smiled at him and he smiled back.

Jan was watching it all from the kitchen and not liking it at all, the pang of jealousy smacked her hard and she stood up walking into the room, marching almost to the centre and looking down at them both where they sat.

"So are you going to tell us who you actually are and how you come to know all these things?" Jan said with a purposely broad hint of distaste in her voice.

"Jan, please understand I mean no harm here, and are only here to help" Sophia said looking up at her and catching her eye.

"Well, no one has ever heard of you, how did you know where to come? In fact where have you come from, and stop staring me in the eyes will you?"

"Jan that is enough, Sophia saved my life and has probably done on numerous occasions a little more tact and compassion might not go amiss" Ray said looking at her.

"It is fine I understand, Jan you are a good woman, a jealous one at the moment but genuinely a good woman, I can see you care for Ray very much, we all do, there is no need for hostility we are all on the same side" Sophia smiled at her.

"I don't, trust you" was Jan's honest answer

"No, I know you don't and why should you? But in time you will come to realise I mean no harm and will only do what is in Ray's best interests"

"Yeah I bet, now if you don't mind I need to look at his dressings"

"Yes of course." Sophia stood up and walked into the kitchen, where Darius offered her a drink which she thankfully accepted.

Jan peeled the dressing off Ray and inspected his wounds they were heeling well and she was pleased, she felt him looking at her and then stopped and sighed staring back at him as if to ask "what".

"Just calm down Jan, she is a good woman and without her I would not be where I am now, so please lose this attitude,

"You have no idea who the hell she is, it is just a bit suspicions to me"

"Actually I have had her with me for many years just had no idea about it, something like Lillian really, she is a guardian of some sort, there is no evil there, no threat, so calm down and please keep your professionalism. I need you, ok?" Ray looked at her and was pleased to see the old Jan return she sighed and nodded, accepting what he was saying finally.

She finished what she was doing and went up stairs for a shower seeming to be more acceptable and calmer but she was a woman, so he would never really know.

Darius was talking to Sophia when Ray eased himself up and came into the kitchen, they both looked at him and he half smiled as he went to make himself some breakfast and they let him do it, knowing he didn't want treating like a child. He had to get himself going and moving.

"So where are you from Sophia? Darius continued to ask, your accent is lovely"

"I am Spanish originally, but live in Yorkshire now, I was sent to expensive finishing schools here in England to rid myself of it but it has not gone completely, she said nodding proudly.

Ray smiled to himself and carried on, he listened to their conversation during his breakfast, without adding to it, Jan came back down and Ray went up for a wash and shave now the swelling was going down a bit on his face. He felt much better after it and took Bodie out to the garden and fed him also. Sophia came up to them both she knelt down and gently stroked Bodie on the head, he didn't mind and licked her hand, something Ray had never seen him do to anyone before.

"You know Jan is in love with you don't you?" she said not looking up at Ray as she said it.

"Oh I don't know, she is just very fond I think"

"No, she loves you, I have seen it in her heart" standing up she faced him and looked him in the eyes once again admiringly; she smiled and tilted her head slightly to the side.

"What is wrong with your neck?" he asked with a slight smile.

"You are one of a kind that is for sure, I always wondered if you would live up to everything, if and when I ever met you, and I must say you have, in fact you have exceeded it, warrior Ray, I will always go on doing whatever I can to help and guard you, you will never be alone, so long as I am alive you will never be alone, I do promise you that"

"You are too kind, and thank you" He tilted his head to match hers which made her smile, then laugh a delightful laugh.

"If you were not so battered and bruised I would hug you" she said.

"If I was not so battered and bruised I would let you" he replied.

Sophia and Ray chatted most of the day, she knew a lot about what he had done and she explained the things she had made happen to help him, what she had reached out into her dreams and altered. Jan came round and calmed to the fact this woman was here.

"I have seen things in my dreams, terrible things and I am not sure what they have meant, things that are going to happen or maybe I am seeing things that have already happened but I see horrid things" Sophia was explaining.

"Don't have to tell me about nightmares" Ray confirmed.

"But these are more I think, much more, premonitions? Or something, I am not sure. Most of the time, I can decipher what I see, but sometimes things come to me. I have no idea what they are, I have been having a dream of darkness, of holes with dwellers in them, of a long lost breed and they are coming Ray, coming from the darkness and you have to be ready, Angelique will not stop, she is pure evil that woman." There was a hint of fear in her voice, masked with worry and disguised with urgency.

"I know I will not fail the next time I meet her, I should of took her out as soon as I first saw her, the fucking bitch" Ray spat his words out like a bad taste

"She can summon darkness, Ray, you have to be ready and you have to be fit, at this moment you are neither, you need time and you must disappear to heal" Sophia was concerned and looked at them all in the room one by one has they all listened to her words.

"I will heal fast I have too always have done, then I will go and hunt her down and destroy her in her lair" Ray sounded confident but was not convincing them in the room, they could see how battered he was and Bodie needed more time to fix.

"No, she will just summon hell fire and you will be gone, and she would of won, please listen to me you must leave here, you must go away and come back to fight another day, it is not a matter of just healing and finding her, you are not just fighting her Ray, you are taking on all the hellish madness she can summon." Sophia looked at him with worry in her eyes.

"She might be right" Darius said

"You need time Ray, you both do" said Jan who had to agree looking at Bodie, who was laid down resting across the room.

"How do I know she won't just follow, what about this place what if she returns here?"

"It is you she is after; it is you she wants, you are a warrior Ray, Warriors are not born they are not made, warriors create themselves through trial and error, pain and suffering and their ability to conquer, you must retreat to fight another day, if you try now you will lose, and I think you know it" Sophia's words filled the room and everyone thought on them for a moment. Ray looked at her, then across at Bodie.

"You must do what is practical" Darius told him

"Your dog needs rest and so do you, it is no use being stubborn about it" Jan said more sternly than usual.

Ray would normally not have of listened, but Sophia's eyes burned into him somehow, he looked at her and agreed, he nodded and looked at Bodie saying.

"Bodie needs time to heal up and get fit, so I will make him good before we go for her"

"I am glad you see sense, now everyone needs to get back to their lives and you need to disappear for a while" Sophia said commandingly.

"How did you know I was here? How did you get here?" Ray asked austerely

Sophia looked at him and frowned a little in confusion; Jan liked the questions and looked at her for an answer intensely.

"I told you, I know all about you I can see what you do in my dreams, in my nightmares, I always know where you are"

"How did you get here so quick?" Ray looked her in the eye and started to read her as she read others, his face was hard and his eyes unyielding.

"There is no need to be cautious of me, I mean you, and cannot do you any harm, you can hone in on the darkness Ray, you always have done, you just know where it is, I am the same with you I am your guardian and can hone in on you at any time"

"If that is so, then maybe you are a liability, if you are captured, tortured, you can always tell them where to find me?"

"If they knew about me, if they knew what I was capable of, which they don't, I can mask myself very well, I would die before giving into them, I would never divulge your whereabouts to anyone"

"That is easy to say, but torture in a very, very nasty thing, it works and has broken the strongest of men, psychologically and physically, it takes a very unique and very tough person to hold out while being tortured"

"What are you saying to me Ray, you do not trust me?" she sounded hurt.

"I am saying all my life I have been cautious, I have had to be, now if you did what you say you did, then I am eternally grateful, if you are who you say you are then I am eternally grateful, but you must understand, I have never seen or heard of you, I did not know you existed, suddenly you are here, I feel no threat from you and my dog feels no evil in you, so that is why we are talking, but if you can mask your actions, your identity what else can you mast, what else can you keep hidden, do you understand what I am saying to you?"

"I think so, but how can I prove myself to you, is that what you need, proof?" she sounded a little taken back, and hurt at his sudden mistrust; he seemed to of changed within a breath.

"Surly she has already done that Ray, proved it by helping you" Darius said not fully understanding Ray's sudden change in direction and opinion of Sophia.

"I have explained all the times I helped you all the times I saw what you were doing, if I was to mean you harm surely I could of done it by now?" Sophia said still looking at Ray and no one else in the room.

"That may be, all the times you talked about have happened, but did you know about them when they were happening or after the event"

"I do not understand this inquisition, I am struggling to understand" Sophia frowned and looked very puzzled.

Ray stood up and went over to his Ouija, he took this to the table sat down and placed the wooden pointer onto it, and he emptied his mind and waited. They watched as something was spelled out and he watched it. He then turned and gestured Sophia to come to him, which she did without question or hesitation.

"Place your fingers lightly on there" Ray said standing up so she could sit in his place, she did as asked and they watched the board. She looked at it and was emotionless. Ray stood back and looked round the room, he seemed to be looking or searching for something, he closed his eyes and then opened them again looking at Bodie. Nothing at all happened, the board did not move, he got no bad feeling or signs, he walked back over to the table and gently lifted her hands off the wooden pointer. She turned and looked at him.

Have I passed the test?" she said a little hurt but trying to understand.

Ray said nothing and went over to Bodie he stroked his dog and made sure he was comfortable; he got him some more fresh water and placed it by his side. He then came back and sat down, in the chair.

"It was not a test as such, more of an observation" he said as she came back and stood in from of him.

"Observation, what did you want to observe?"She questioned

"You" he smiled very slightly and then looked at everyone else, in the room.

"Ok who is going to offer to make a brew?"

"I nominate Jan" Darius said

"I second it, thanks Jan you are a star" Ray told her.

"Cheeky Bastards" she said and stood up going into the kitchen to make a tea.

Sophia shook her head and stared at Ray for a moment then went and sat down herself.

"Don't take it personal" Ray said not looking at her.

"I am not, just trying to understand why you don't trust me after all we have discussed?"

"I trust no one, and it is safer for me that way, I know you are not a threat but I also know you can mask your actions very well" he lifted his eyes and looked at her.

"I have to, it is much safer for me, that way" she said looking straight back at him.

"There you go then" he said holding her stare.

She eventually shyly smiled and nodded and accepted what he was saying.

The atmosphere was quieter and Sophia felt a little uncomfortable Ray had taken her back a little and she tried and did understand why he had talked and chatted to make her at ease, and then test her to see what her reaction would be. She understood it but she just had this admiration for him she didn't understand, she knew about him knew what he had done and been through, but when she actually met him and looked into his piercing blue eyes, she lost a bit of her self control.

Ray grin and bared the pain when Jan changed his dressings cleaning the wounds up and checking on the stitching they were sore and painful but had begun to heal, she was happy with them, Ray was stiff and he ached he took pain killers, but they didn't do much good to take the pain away. His head thumped, his body ached and his wounds stung but he was alive and he was on his feet. He was more concerned about Bodie than himself. He checked on him checked his stitches also, Bodie moved slowly and carefully the only way his ribs were going to fix was with quiet and rest. Ray knew he had to get away and recover; he could not fight or defend anyone at the moment. He also knew if they found him he would be in trouble, he needed a safe place a hidden place, and maybe Sophia could provide that place?

Ray went and had a strip wash he could not really get into the shower with his wounds and bandages, he had trouble shaving too so didn't bother, his face was still swollen but the yellowing was coming out, his body ached and was stiff but he kept it moving and stretching as much as he dared, he could feel himself mending and the wounds healing, he was gaining strength all the time, he ate well and drank well too, he always healed quickly, he had to, his mind set was strong and he never gave into pain or discomfort. He slept in the bed that night and got some good rest. Sophia stayed the night and it was yet again John who stayed up looking out for everyone has they slept.

The next morning Ray was up early, he and Bodie were in the garden strolling round he was giving Bodie a little exercise and seeing how he was coping, they both seemed better and were gaining strength. They were always better together and would heal quicker if they did it together gaining strength from each other.

After a very large hearty full English breakfast he had for dinner in the mid afternoon, Ray started to pack a bag with his things, Jan had given him some spare medical supplies and bandages she had instructed Sophia how to take the stitches out after a week, she instructed her on what to look for if there was any infection and what to do if there were. Sophia listened and took in what she was told. Bodie's wounds were checked and cleaned, he also needed looking after, but Ray would see to that, soon they were set. Darius shook Ray's hand and a little longer than he needed to do, he looked him in the eye and Ray just smiled and nodded to him, nothing else needed to be said, Darius would always be there without question.

Jan hugged him carefully and kissed him in the same way, he held her and kept holding her a little longer and whispered a "thank you" in her ear she nodded and held back her tears.

John shook Rays hand and smiled.

"Look after them big lad, I owe you" Rays said with sincerity

I will do my best Ray" he said

Sophia said her good buys while Ray packed the car and got Bodie gingerly in to the back seat and made him comfortable. Everything was set and he sat in the driver's seat making sure he could actually drive alright, it pained him a little but he was ok with it.

Sophia got into the passenger's seat and put her seat belt on, Ray looked back in his mirror and saw them all standing watching them go, he just hoped he was not leaving them in danger but he knew he had to get away to recover and mend, if he was not there then maybe they were safe, he hoped so anyway.

"Directions" Ray said looking at Sophia,

"Well Ray it is a place you know only too well, a place you have visited many times and somewhere that we have been that close I could have touched you"

"Same question" Ray said waiting patiently

"Skipton, north Yorkshire" she said without further ado

"I know it well, near Bolton Abbey which I also know well" he said driving away and remembering the adventure he had there some years ago with the dark prince and that almost killed him at that time too.

Sophia knew what he meant and nodded, she settled in the seat and glanced back at Bodie who was almost asleep already he needed rest and he was making sure he got it.

"If you need me to drive or you feel too much pain just let me know, I don't mind driving" she threw the question at him and left it there, he said nothing but heard her and understood. There was no way she was going to drive him of course while he was fit he would drive his own car, but the gesture was noted.

They sped on and he then checked his fuel it was full and should get them there ok, so there were no worries about that. Ray would have gone the whole way in silence it wouldn't of bothered him one bit. Sophia probably would too but after about half hour they just started to talk, it was not rushed it was not forced it just happened together out of the blue as if the one was waiting for the other one to start the conversation.

"How do you make your money, how do you make a living I mean" Ray started

"My father is a very rich man back in Spain, he owns several magazines I have an allowance off him and he bought me this house some years ago I am very lucky really"

"Yes you are, so what the hell do you do all day?" Ray spoke without taking his eyes off the road and he constantly checked his mirror, constantly made mental notes of vehicles and cars around him and behind him, he never let his guard down and trusted nothing or no one, he always locked the doors from the inside and kept a keen eye on the road.

"I work for charity, some shop work and some online work for them, it keeps me busy and I enjoy it also of course"

"So basically you do sod all and live off your dad's money" Ray said bluntly but not offensively although it might have sounded so.

"If you want to put it that way" she said quietly

"I am not being odious just saying that's all"

"I would hate to meet you when you were then" she smiled at him and laughed.

"Good on you, better than working for a living, so where is this house of yours and how big is it, what is the surrounding area like, are be backed onto any fields, are we near a road, is there off road parking" Ray reeled off the questions as if they were all one.

"Bloody hell, ermm, yes we have off road parking, the house is detached four bed rooms quite large, set back from the road, we are just at the north side of the town we can see the castle from the bed room window, fields to the rear but we have a sizable garden"

"I will check the place out when we get there, I think I know where you are, and does the canal run not too far from you?"

"Yes that is right I walk down to it and along the bank sometimes" she looked at him and smiled at the thought of the lovely peaceful evenings she had done so, but Ray's face was more stern and he was asking for more security reasons than thinking of evening strolls.

"What are your doors and windows made of are the still wooden frames, do they have internal locks on them, and do you have any out buildings?"

"We will be safe Ray I will make sure of that, I will do all in my power to keep us undetected and secure" she looked at him and said her words with authority and confidence.

"Yes, I am sure you will but I still like to do some checks, just in case you know, and please answer me how did you travel down this way from Skipton?" there was no hint of distrust in his voice but the question wanted answering.

"Yes of course, and I used my car, we can pick that up when we go back I will use it to come home again, I talked to Darius about it and he said he would look after it for me"

"Really, he never mentioned it"

"You are welcome to ring him and ask" she was calm and unconcerned and it satisfied Ray but he would still ring and ask Darius later.

"Food, I hope you are not one of these vegetarian types, I like real food, meat and things nothing wrong with real food"

"You will be well fed Ray, do not worry, and Bodie too, the whole point of this is to build you both up and make you both strong again"

"Yes, that's good then" he shifted in his seat and pulled a face at the pain shooting through his shoulder where he stretched a little too much and the stitches pulled, he ached and his head was starting to pump again.

"You ok, do you want some tablets, or me to drive?" she asked already knowing the answer.

"No, I will be fine" he carried on and drove fast but steady; she didn't need to give him any directions he knew where he was going.

CHAPTER SEVEN

Darius and Jan had got the place back to where it should be, tidied up and cleaned, John cleared up outside and got rid of any evidence Ray had ever been there, they were not sure what else to do, Jan had to get back to her work, she was not happy another woman was looking after her warrior, but she had to accept it, and she would never forget the time they spent together, and besides he was coming back. Darius was playing everything close to his chest, keeping his real thoughts hidden but keeping calm within the circle of friends. John was just glad to help; he would never turn Darius down and would always be there for him, no matter what. They all went about what they had to do. The place seemed empty somehow, quiet and as if something big and all consuming had gone, leaving a void. Jan said her farewells and left to get back to her life the best she could. She and Darius were going to ring each other every day and night to make sure they were safe. John was asked to stay with Darius for a while longer also.

The car Sophia travelled down in was put away in the lock up garage and kept safe Darius had taken her number and given his to her so she could keep them informed, things were getting back to normal, or so it seemed.

Quietly watching high up in a large oak tree in a neighbouring garden were a pair of eyes that had been watching everything for the past two days and nights, it was a small dweller from the underground of the woods, sent to spy on the house, and tonight under the cover of darkness it would run and hurry back undetected and report what it had seen.

Back along the trees, in the shrubs along the road side, across the fields, keeping low and out of sight, eventually getting back into the woods and down one of the many tunnels it knew all too well, reporting back to she who had sent it, Angelique looking drained, and pale, her face twisted hideously in pain. she was hunched over and sat in the darkness, quiet and still, the dweller came cautiously up to her and they communicated, she understood what it was telling her and she rocked her head back, the gaping holes in her shoulders had deformed her arms and they looked awkward and twisted hanging from the shoulders. She looked more like dweller of the tunnels then she did anything else. Her eyes were semi closed, she could just make out things in the darkness, just movements and she could smell the rotting filth around her, they had saved her life but she had paid a horrid price for it. She settled back and hunched over once again, her pain was immense, her wounds taking longer to heal. But she would heal and she would have revenge, the next time she would not fail.

Ray was pulling the car onto the large driveway and stopped right outside the door, he did not get out of the car he had a good look round the gravelled area, all the garden had been gravelled off and made into a low maintenance garden. He looked at the large house its red brick construction looked old but sturdy, he knew houses were built to last in those days.

Sophia stretched and opened the door, all the locked clicked open as she pulled the lever releasing the central locking Ray always engaged when driving. She got out and took a deep breath of evening air. It was dark and very quiet, just the way she liked it. They had not stopped and drove here in one go. Ray eased his stiff body out of the car and stretched carefully; he then opened the back door and helped Bodie to ease just as careful, out of the car. Bodie got going and tentatively stretched himself, then sniffed about and marked the spot.

Sophia came up to Ray, looked at the house, then at him saying.

"Well will it do? It has four bedrooms, a down stairs toilet and fully fitted kitchen, it is warm and cosy and secure. I like it and live here quite happily"

"It looks nice, but it is only as secure as its weakest point" Ray walked to the back of the car and started to unpack. She went to the blue wooden oversized door and unlocked it, she pushed it open and went inside, Ray saw some lights come on down stairs and the curtains pulled and drawn, Bodie slowly came up to him and stood by his side, Ray reached down and gently stroked the dogs head. Sophia came out and helped him inside with some of the bags he had. Ray locked the car up and they all went inside, locking the door behind them.

Within twenty minutes Darius had been rung and told they were safe, Ray had a mug of tea and a barrel of biscuits by his side, he was sat on a black leather settee, his feet resting up on a matching stool it was a very comfortable house, Sophia was sat on a large bean bag in the corner, it looked stupid to Ray but she seemed to be content to sit in it looking awkward. Bodie had been fed and watered and he was laid on his side on a fur rug in front of a real open fireplace which was not lit. Ray dunked a biscuit and ate it in one mouthful. Sophia watched him and smiled.

"Yeah it's a nice big house, you have made it look nice, simple decor not too complicated, more of what you need and not cluttered" he said looking round the large but simple room.

"Glad you approve, I like to live simply, really don't see the point of a lot of things you don't need or use, dust gathers" she shifted her position and the bean bag moved with her moulding itself to her shape and settling down as she was still again.

"You comfortable in that thing? It looks bloody stupid to me" Ray said taking a gulp of tea

"It is very comfortable thanks, you should try one" she smiled knowing what he was going to say and his face he would pull.

"You can't get out of the bloody things when you sit on them, no, I will make do with a chair thanks or a settee"

"You never know unless you try" she said with a smile, she felt more at ease and comfortable in her own home, he own domain and most of all, she felt safe.

"I will make the spare room up for you, in a few minutes, you look tired Ray, and I need to check your dressings and wounds"

"I am fine, I want to walk round the house first get a feel of it, see where everything is feel its vibes sort of speak, do you have a loft and if so is it boarded out so you can walk up there, is there a cellar?"

"No we don't have a cellar, and the loft is all floored yes, nothing up there though, let me do your dressings and then you can go and explore I will leave you to it"

Ray said nothing while she changed his dressings the wounds were healing well and knitting together, the stitches could come out soon and he would not need the dressings on them. She made a good job and then let him explore the house, get the feel of it, see it's lay out, he spent about half an hour walking round and looking out of each window, checking everything he needed to check, looking out each window, at the approaches leading to it, looking up in the loft the four bed rooms were simply decorated and he liked the place, much too big for one person but what the hell, she didn't pay for it.

Sophia made up the spare room, Ray went back down to let Bodie out and make sure he had food and drink, he locked the doors and double checked them and the windows too, he turned off the lights and went up to bed, he brushed his teeth and they all settled down for the night.

It was silent outside and Ray liked the place, he lay in bed and just listened trying to pick up slight sounds from outside, he smiled when he heard an owl hoot its call somewhere round the back of the house. He closed his eyes and drifted off to sleep.

Bodie was awake and listening he had sensed no danger but he was still on guard no matter what his condition. The pain in his side was easing day by day but he still had to be careful he had a lot of healing to do. He eventually closed his eyes and went to sleep too, the house was quiet, still and for this night at least it was safe.

A big hearty breakfast was waiting for Ray when he got up, he washed, carefully, and went down stairs to the smell of bacon and other fine smells drifting from the kitchen, he saw Bodie sat next to Sophia being given treats as she cooked the food, a little off cut of bacon, a small sausage, he waited and ate them all. Looking round his tail wagged at the sight of Ray, who came into the kitchen and stroked his dog.

"Jan said you lost a lot of blood and need feeding, you do not look as pale as you did at least, and I am making you a full breakfast" she said not looking up at him.

"That will do nicely, looks like Bodie is doing ok as well"

"I have been feeding him a few little bits until his is ready, hope that is ok" she looked up from her cooking for a moment.

"Its fine, have you let him out yet?"

"He went out round the back earlier for ten minutes sniffing everything and pissing on just about everything as well actually"

"He is getting better then, my bloody stitches are itching" he circled his shoulders and started to scratch at one of his wounds.

"Don't do that you silly arse, if they are itching they are healing, just leave them alone, sit down it will be ready in a few minutes, I have made you a mug of tea, it's there on the table"

Ray sat down and took as sip of his tea, he then scratched at one of his wounds again not letting her see him do so. He did feel better and was getting stronger and less stiff as each day went by, he was pleased to see Bodie moving about a bit too. The food smelled delicious and he was made hungrier by the smell, she looked content and happy enough cooking it for him and he yawned and then smiled at Bodie as he got another little tidbit.

Later that day they went for a walk, Bodie was told to stay which he did but was not happy about, they walked down past the road and by the canal; Ray had been here before and knew the place pretty well. Some people looked at his battered but healing face but made no comment, the market town did get quite busy some day's but today it was not too bad, walking round did him good got him moving and the fresh air felt good in his lungs.

They walked over the small bridge and Ray stopped, looking at the two canal barges, moored up by the sand/bank. Sophia stood by his side.

"They have one with a restaurant on it you know, you can have lunch and travels up and down the canal while you eat"

"Yeah I know, must be a peaceful life living on one of them, but freezing in winter don't you think, not really a man of the water myself"

"Well it suits some people; they spend their whole life on them"

"Everyone to their own I suppose, but looks to me you are stuck in a long tube bit like a sardine, too claustrophobic for my liking, but I suppose you can travel to some very nice places" He turned and looked at the ducks idling on the water waiting for the next person to throw them some bread, a seagull perched on a ledge above waiting to swoop down and steal whatever it could. He looked round and was lost in his thoughts for a moment; Sophia stood patiently and figured he was remembering the last time he was here, when ever that was.

"It is a nice place here and there is the dales just on my door step of course, very beautiful places to explore and walk" she said finally.

"Well it's the Yorkshire dales love, of course it is." he smiled at her then moved on down the road, "Is that pub still here that has that roaring open fire and serves pretty good grub?"

"The Peacock, yes it is, do you want to go and have some lunch?"

"I will have to give you some money, it is going to cost you a fortune to have me and Bodie here, not fair on you is it"

"Don't talk stupid, I don't want any money, you are here to get fit and well and I will see to it that you both do, money is not an issue, so no more about that please"

"If you insist but I still think I should contribute"

"Shut up" she said smiling at him just in case he didn't take it as it was meant.

They headed down the cobbled streets that lead into the high street, more people were here, hurrying on their way, most with their heads down and not wanting to be bothered.

They walked round the town and then had some lunch, did some shopping for supplies and dog food, walked back and up the hill to her house, Ray greeted Bodie as he came up to the door as soon as they got in, he then went and fed him and let him out into the garden.

Darius rang Sophia and so did Jan, she reported to them what was happening and how things were going, they all seemed happy and nothing else had happened at their end either. The night fell in and the darkness came quickly, Ray had a walk around the outside of the house with Bodie before they locked up and settled in.

Bodie was lay by the back door and was alert but all was calm, Ray lay in bed his hands clasped behind his head and looking up at the ceiling, Sophia had just got into her comfy bed and settled down, she laid on her side the covers pulled up over her shoulders and snuggled in, she loved her bed and considered one of her favourite things. She was thinking of Ray, she was thinking thoughts she shouldn't but couldn't help it, eventually she closed her eyes and fell into a thoughtful sleep.

The days passed into weeks and the weeks into months and Ray became stronger and more intense she could noticed he was becoming restless, Bodie was gaining strength he was going for long walks with Ray building his strength and they were looking more like them old selves each day that passed. She had done a great job looking after them but she could tell Ray was becoming more and more uncomfortable, she backed off and left him to go for his walks, eventually early morning runs, he did exercises and stretches and he became more and more withdrawn more private, and less talkative. He was getting ready and she knew it, he checked with his Ouija often. Had long bouts of sitting in silence, deep in thought maybe, she was not sure. He had healed fast, had more scars but it seemed not to bother him, he had something on his mind and she knew not to interfere, but was concerned. She was doing all in her power to protect him but even she was beginning to feel something strange, like she was being attacked or assaulted it was a very strange and worrying feeling. Her dreams became more vivid and disturbing; she had sudden bouts of palpitations and anxiety, something she had not experienced before.

One morning she awoke early and looked out of the window the sun was only just rising and the day beginning, it was cool but dry, she looked out across the field then down to where she saw Ray at his car, and he had everything out and lay on the ground, going through his supplies. She sighed and knew the time was very close to him going and leaving, she had not known what to expect while he was with her, but she had hopes and she had felt a lot of feelings for him. But although he was appreciative and positive he never showed any emotional liking for her, she had not really known if he was just being a gentleman and had values and manners or if he didn't like her that way, or maybe he just had too much on his mind. She watched him go through his things and pack them back into the car, Bodie was sniffing about and keeping a watchful eye, he looked and was fully recovered; the fur had grown back where he had been shaved for the operation. He looked meaner and leaner than ever and so did Ray. They had eaten well and got back into shape she smiled to herself and knew what she had done had been instrumental in that fact; she had done a good job. She would go on protecting him as and when she could. She silently watched him and looked as how he moved, how nothing seemed to bother him, even after the dramatic events that had happened, even though he almost died, he just seemed to bounce back, adjust and carry on, she could not help but admire him. When he had finished he walked back into the house, she came down the stairs dressed in an oversize and buttoned shirt that came down to her knees and joined him in the kitchen.

He looked up and smiled at her, he walked towards her and put his arms on her shoulders and looked her in the eye, she was slightly taken back and didn't know what was going to happen, and she hoped he would kiss her.

"Just want to take this opportunity to thank you for all you have done Sophia, you have looked after us very well and I am in your debt, if there is every anything I can do for you please do not hesitate to ask, you are a wonderful and very special girl, but I cannot put you in any more danger, there are forces attacking you and sooner or later they will get through and your peace here will be gone and shattered. I am leaving and will take you back down to pick up your car rom Darius I will get you some money for my keep also"

She nodded and felt the lump in her throat rising, she took a deep and brave breath, and didn't know why she was feeling like this, looking him in the eye she smiled and nodded again.

"I understand, there is no need for the money you silly man, but please promise me you will be more than careful, you are not indestructible Ray, they will come for you again and Angelique can summon for hell, she is not dead I can feel her evil still"

"I know she is not, and that is why I have to go, I do not want you in any more danger and she is looking for you, looking for me, searching and sending out hunters, sooner or later they will get through and find me, I want her destroyed before she gains an militia and any more strength" his eyes looked into hers deeply, he smiled and she smiled back, she knew the kiss was coming and she welcomed it. He kissed her softly then again with more passion, stopping slowly he pulled away and smiled at her.

"You are a very unique man Ray Sibson, and it has been a pleasure to serve" she said smiling back at him, not losing eye contact.

"I would like to come and visit you, repay you for your kindness, maybe when all this is over, or when I am in these parts again?"

"Welcome anytime, when are you going, today?"

"Yes we need to get this finished and over with, I am not wanting to come across another fucking thing like last time, so will burn the bitch out"

"Shall I get dressed and we can go now then?"

"Hell no let's have breakfast and a cuppa first at least, I am starving, why don't you go have a shower and get dressed I will cook us breakfast"

"Well that is an offer I cannot refuse" she smiled and turned going back up stairs, but had sadness in her heart knowing this was the last day she would be spending with him, she had come accustomed to having him around, and it surprised her somewhat because she always liked her own space and solitude.

Ray cooked them a good breakfast and got showered himself afterwards. He double checked his car and supplies he made sure Bodie was watered and fed. He was ready to go and Sophia locked the house securing everything and double checked all the doors and windows. She got into the car and fastened her seat belt, looking back she felt a little sad knowing when she came back she would be back alone and it would be like it was before he came.

Ray filled his car up at the petrol station and they headed off he did not speak much and she didn't push any conversation. They drove steady she kept glancing across at Ray every now and then but he seemed to be miles away. Until a motor bike cut him up and raced on past him in the middle of the road.

"Fucking wanker, they are a pain in the arse them twats" Ray said spitting his words out

"He will come off the bloody thing one day and get his comeuppance" Sophia added.

"Think they own the bloody road, feel like ramming the tossers off the road"

It broke the ice sort of speak and they chatted more on their way down, she felt more at ease and comfortable in the car now they were talking. The journey seemed to go quicker and they were there before she knew it. No one was home but Ray knew Darius had left him a key in a secret place, it was always there just in case he every needed it, a very trusting man Darius with Ray anyway.

Bodie was let out and he immediately went on his rounds of the area, sniffing marking and checking. Ray went into the house followed by Sophia who made them a drink while Ray phoned Darius to inform him of his arrival.

CHAPTER EIGHT

The dark damp hole where Angelique had spent these weeks had been torture for her, she was deformed, her wounds not healed very quickly or well, she could not move her arms as she wanted, they seemed to be twisted the wrong way, she was in constant pain and was dirty and filthy, although the dwellers had saved her life, she had become more their slave and captive rather than their leader, getting scraps of food from them she felt helpless and angry, she still had her power to summon and she would use it as soon as she had chance. She had summoned phantoms to search for Ray but so far nothing had been picked up, he was being protected and protected very well. She struggled to move and had been cramped up and hunched in this dark hole for weeks, it stunk and she was only now being about to move a bit. She cursed as she struggled in the darkness about the dirty floor, she scrambled up a small shaft and it opened out into a bigger area, every now and then she heard the grunt of a dweller by her side, or in front of her, they could see quite well but she was blind in this darkness. The jolt in her body and arms was sending shock waves of pain though her body but she carried on, noticing the air becoming easier to breath, she must be near an opening she thought, lifting her head she struggled to look round and try and see some sort of light. Her arms were painful but she could at least move them now, not giving her much support but some at least. She laid on her back feeling exhausted, taking deep breaths and then rolling over and up to her knees straining her eyes she looked round and then lifted her head she could smell cleaner air, a slight draft, she turned her head to the side and followed her nose, yes, the air was more fresh here, she kept going crawling up and along a narrow chamber that rose slightly onto another level and here she could see faint beams of light coming from above. She laid back and took deeper breaths of air. It was good to breath cleaner air and it picked her spirit up instantly. The light was seeping in from above, small beams from the side of the inner wall; it must have been some sort of exit. She laid there and got her breath and strength back.

Two dwellers came by her side and looked down at her, they grunted and knelt by her side, more keeping an eye on her than protecting her, she was not sure how they actually saw her now, she had come to them as a leader and controller, but she now felt trapped and their prisoner. She lay there and breathed easier the air that was coming in from above, her eyes had accustomed a little to the light that was piecing the darkness and she began to make out where she was, she could see the outline of the dwellers by her side she looked round the small cavern like space and knew she was near the surface. She was weak and dirty and needed food and water and desperately to clean up but she was not too concerned about that right now she wanted to find out where Ray was and she needed more help. Her idea was to wait until dark then go up into the night air, and summon her hunters and shadow forces to find him and then she would destroy him once and for all. Her hatred for him had become tenfold and she wanted him destroyed, drawn and quartered. This is what gave her strength and determination to go on. And anyone in her way would be disposed of, and treated with the same contempt and hatred. She got herself up and sat on the ground, looking up at the small beams of light shining through, she lifted her head and smelled the cleaner air of the outside, blinking her eyes that had been in the dark for so long, she peered at the small bit of light like it was a life line, a chance of some sort. Kneeling up she stretched her limbs out they were stiff and painful but it felt good to be able to stretch her legs fully out for a change and to be able to twist and turn her body to get the circulation and feeling back somewhat. But she was saddened about her arms, not being able to lift them very well or use them as she wanted, they gave her a little support but not much, but she hoped they would heal eventually and get more strength in them as time went on. Arching her back she lifted her head and smelled the cleaner air, filling her lungs with it and trying to forget the stench of the lower passageways and caverns where she had been for many weeks, But which seemed like years. She was going to go out this evening into the clean night air and she couldn't wait.

"Ray, where the hell are you, you sexy beast" Jan shouted as she came into the house at full speed, she came dashing over as soon as Darius had phoned her to tell her Ray was back. Her face was full of happiness and eagerness and she looked round as she marched into the house searching for him. She then came face to face with Sophia who stopped her in her tracks, her face dropped for a moment then she smiled a gain but nowhere as wide as she was before.

"Hello Sophia where is Ray?" she asked looking over her shoulder and past and searching with her eyes into the living room.

"He is in the garden with his dog" Sophia said and watched Jan march out the back and greet Ray, she watched her from the kitchen window has she threw herself at him and hugged him, then stood back and looked him over. Sophia could not really hear what they were saying and she was not really interested at this moment.

She bowed her head and sighed, she didn't really know what to expect of Ray he had made her happy, curious and sad, he had made her angry, forgiving and critical, in fact he had brought just about every feeling and emotion she had, and not once had he tried to make a pass at her or take advantage. She looked up and knew she was feeling jealously, but she had to pull herself together she still had to carry on protecting him whenever she could, this was her destiny and quest in life, a gift and chore that had been put upon her without choice. She quietly shifted away and went out to find her car.

"You are looking well Ray, my god you are looking well" Jan said looking him up and down, standing back a little more to admire him.

"I don't really feel a hundred percent but I am getting there, there will be time to heal later I have to get this job finished and finished now"

"It is a bloody miracle, you look a thousand times better than you did the last time I saw you it is amazing how fast you bounce back, bloody amazing"

"It's all in the reflexes, and mind over matter you have to stay positive, to get a positive result" Ray said looking at her with a little smile on his face.

"Bloody miracle, if I had not seen it with my own eyes I would of said it impossible, that beating should of killed you and very nearly did, I thought you would be paralysed for life, just do not understand, but what the hell, it is you and you are always surprising me"

Ray saw Sophia walking towards the garage at the side of the house, he excused himself from Jan and walked over to her, and she had gone into the garage and was opening the doors wide so she could drive her car out.

"You were going without saying farewell?" Ray asked her leaning on the garage door.

"I thought you were busy, she nodded towards Jan without looking in her direction.

"Silly arse, I hope there is not a pang of jealously there, why don't you wait, Darius will be back soon and he would like to see you no doubt"

"No, I will get going I have a long drive, I am not needed here now" she had her head bowed and opened the car door.

"I will not stop you, but I will ask you once to not go yet, you can rest up and go tomorrow, I owe you a lot and want you to realise and know that fact"

She looked up at him and kept his stare for a moment, then tilted her head as if it has just been dropped on one side.

"Can I ask you something?" she said looking him straight in the eye.

"Of course" he returned her stare and would not pull away from it.

"You never made a pass at me, not once, I understand you were in a bad way and all that but the last few week you have been almost back to your fighting weight and shape, but not once did you make a play for me, I am just not your type?"

"You know. Women in general normally piss me off, you never know where the hell you have them or you just can't do right for doing wrong, I have no emotion attachment to them, but to be honest with you, I do find you very attractive, not only physically but also spiritually you have a very strong mind, and a very strong will I do admire that, I do not respect many people, least of all daft women, but I do respect you, and when this is all over I would like to come back to your house and thank you for all you have done, I now consider you a friend and ally, I do not have many really so I would appreciate it"

She gazed at him and her face showed no emotion for a while she thought about what he had said, she then thought about whom she was talking to, and a small smile came across her face and straighten her head again and took a deep breath.

"You are a bastard, but I would like to be your friend yes, thank you, I would consider it a great honour and will do my best to help you"

"It is not a honour darling it is something we can build, appreciate and cherish, to have a true friend is a very rare and wonderful thing, and I will be do all I can to protect you if the need every arises, I owe you much and will not forget it I can assure you of that"

"I believe you" she said smiling and feeling much better for some reason.

"Right go put the kettle on let's have a brew and you are staying until tomorrow"

He walked away and she followed closing the garage doors behind her.

That evening they were all sat round in Darius's front Room, Ray had set down his plan of action and they were milling over it.

Jan was sat next to Sophia who now was a lot more comfortable with Jan, Darius was sat next to John, and Bodie and Ray were together on the settee.

"It will take a lot of petrol Ray, a lot and you don't know how many they are, the tunnels could run for miles" Darius said

"I don't think there is that many, and yes the tunnels could run for miles but I want that bitch out in the open, I will pour petrol down the entrances I know about set the fuckers on fire, the smoke will travel through the tunnels and rise at other exits I will then pour petrol down these too and just burn the bitch out"

"I know but what if she just exits through another hole and is gone while you are still there" Jan said taking a sip of her brandy.

"She wants me dead, I think her rage will control her, she will have to be there to summon whatever she needs to fight me, and so I will use that to my advantage. As soon as I kill her, the others will not know what to do and scatter, I am thinking"

"I don't know, it is very dangerous Ray" Darius said shaking his head.

"Welcome to my world, there is no easy way to do this, she is down under ground, I am betting she will be with them fucking things that live there, I need to get her out into the open, I cannot go down after her, there is just no room to do so, I have to burn her out"

"It is going to set the whole forest on fire, what will happen when the Emergency services arrive?" John said looking round the room hoping what he has said was not stupid.

"Good point you cannot just set the place on fire and not expect people to come running" Jan added nodding at John who felt better with his question now.

"If I pour the petrol down the holes and set it on fire it will just burn underground, it is just to get them out into the open isn't it" Ray corrected them.

"Could do with mustard gas" Darius added dryly and without expression.

"Could you not seal the tunnels, seal them in, that way they will be only a few places they can get out, is there now way of caving them in?" Sophia added.

"It is the same difference, sealing them off or cutting off their exit, the plan is to get them out in the open and disorganised, I need her in sight I cannot just have her doing her stuff underground out of way and me left out in the open"

"I understand that Ray, but what is to say while you are there she is not somewhere else sending whatever she likes to come for you?" Sophia said.

"I will know she is there, I will check with my Board and will sense the bitch she has a strong stench, that one"

"Have you considered smoke bombs and flares?" Darius said looking across at Ray. Everyone then looked at Darius.

"Will they be any good, strong enough?" Ray enquired, but was thinking about it.

"I have some in the shop, they get used for things like paintball weekends and such, but if you let them go in a very confined space it will blind and make it hard to breath and then follow with a flare it will be unbearable. They would have to come out I think"

"But the problem stays the same; I do not know where they are exactly and if they will not just run to another tunnel"

"How about we do the bloody lot, you set them on fire I will smoke them out, just throw everything thing down the bloody hole and see what comes out?" Darius suggested.

Ray liked the simplistic nature of it, but didn't like the fact Darius was going to be there, and then John turned and said.

"I would like to help, the smoke will have to escape somewhere and it will show where the exits and entrances are"

Ray smiled, not pointing out he had already made this fact clear earlier, he sighed stood up and walked round the room thinking to himself. Bodie watched him from the settee.

"Darius have you any gas canisters, or butane bottles?" Ray asked

"A few, but they will go up with a fucking bang Ray, bring curious eyes, don't you think?"

"How about we turn them on throw them down the hole, the smell of gas may spook them to get out of the underground tunnels and into the open, even if they did go up they would be deep underground, muffled and cause a lot of damage down there, like a fucking bomb" He was liking the idea the more he thought about it. Walking to the middle of the room he looked at Darius, who looked back at him with a nod.

"Have several smaller bottles in the garden shed , they are not all full but it will do the trick for what you want I think, I will get you the flares and smoke bombs too, might as well go for the whole lot, if one doesn't work the others might"

"If it gets them out and disorganised then that is what I am after I will go for the bitch as soon as I see her, not give her a chance to do anything"

"There is no light in there Ray if you go at night how the hell you going to be able to see anything, I mean you are in the middle of a forest for god's sake" Jan suddenly said.

"Go at dawn, just as light is breaking, there will be no one about then either" Darius suggested.

Sophia stayed quiet she was watching and listening, although she initially joined in at first she now understood they were talking and planning on killing someone, and although she understood who and what it was, it was still strange to her to see Ray making plans and discussing how to destroy someone, she found it a little unsettling and could not understand why, she had seen and known all about what Ray does for years but to actually watch him plan it so coldly and callously was a bit unnerving to her.

She eventually excused herself and went up stairs out of the way, Jan watched her go and bite her bottom lip thinking she knew what the problem was. Ray was still talking with Darius and didn't take much notice either way. Eventually Jan stood up and quietly went up stairs to find Sophia she searched in the main bed room and saw she was sat on the bed still and quiet, she went in and sat next to her.

"You OK? She said putting her hand on her shoulder.

"Yes, I am fine; it is just a little intense that's all"

"Well he is a very intense person isn't he "

"I have witnessed much and seen much in my dreams, but to be here and see it for real and they are planning to go and destroy someone I mean I know who she is and what she is, it is not that, it is just the thought of how they can cold heartedly,,," she stopped and shook her head and sighed.

"I think I know what you mean, but Ray is a Warrior that is what Warriors do, it is no good thinking he will be tamed or he is like other men, he will never be like that, he will go out and kill and destroy, then switch it off and then that is what you see, someone who looks like and sounds like a normal human being, but believe me, he is not, I have seen him in action a few times and he is far from a normal human being I can assure you of that fact, seeing it first hand is much different than living it in a dream darling"

"Yes I know and I should not let it bother me, but just seeing him one minute, then he is a cold hearted killer the next, take some getting used too"

"You said you had seen it all and helped him in the past, you must of know what he was like, what a sort of man he was?"

"I did, but when I was looking after him when he was battered and injured, he seemed like a different person but now he is back into the killing machine I use to see in my dreams"

"You are a sensitive soul my dear and you have let your emotions get the better of your judgment I think, where is this woman who came here some months ago all positive and sure and confident, reality bites and sometimes gives you a slap in the face doesn't it"

"Yes I know I am being silly but it was a very strong feeling for a little while then, and I just needed to get away from its intensity I think"

"Are you alright now is it subsiding any?"

"Yes it is alright, don't worry, I will be going tomorrow anyway"

"You are welcome here to sat as long as you want you should know that by now"

"I will be fine, thank you for your concern Jan" she smiled at her.

"You have done what a lot of women do, you have fallen for the rough bastard" she smiled back and shook her shoulder playfully pushing her away.

"You think so?" Sophia smiled and they both hugged for a short while and both felt better for each other and for themselves.

The plans went on and Ray wanted to go and get it done there and then, but Darius talked him out of it, simple because he had to go collect the items they needed the next day. Ray decided to go for the full lot, throw everything down the hole and hope it draws them out.

He was happier now he had a plan of sorts, knowing it all could and probably would change when he got there but at least he was now ready. He sharpened his knives that night and made it clear to everyone he was to go alone, he did not want to risk any of them getting captured or used as a hostage, there could be a lot of things running about and he wanted to be able to be free to kill whatever moved it would be easier for him to not have to worry or watch out for anyone else. They all argued but knew it was useless to do so, and he would not move on his decision.

The night was still and quiet but no one got much sleep they all had their own reasons, whether it be a concern or a fear, but it was a restless night. The next morning Ray was up early, he was in the Garden shed with Darius they had found two gas bottles, more than half full these were used for camping stoves, and contained butane gas, put the two red bottles in his car boot, he double checked his Zippo lighter worked. Darius went to his shop to pick up the flares and the smoke bombs. Ray remembered all them years ago he was coming through here with Christine and spotted the shop that Darius owns, he went in to buy arrows that day for his cross bow. How they have come a long way in the years that have passed, Darius had been a very good man and very helpful many times, he never questioned or shied away when Ray needed him, he didn't like to put on him so much but he always sorted out whatever was asked of him and Ray knew he was now a very important part of things.

Sophia quietly got up and showered and dressed, she had a lite breakfast and watched Ray for a little while getting ready. She sighed and walked outside, putting a very brave face on she marched up to him smiling.

"Ok you be bloody careful and know I will be doing all I can to help you Ray" she said standing next to him looking into the Pandora's Box that was the boot of his car.

He put his arm round her and hugged her tight and close to him, she hugged him back and looked up into his blue eyes. He smiled and kissed her gently on the forehead.

"You drive carefully and take care of yourself I will come and see you when all this is over, just be very aware you are under attack so be diligent on your drive back ok?"

"Of course, and you be diligent and make sure you come out of this in one piece, please be careful and take care of yourself"

They hugged again and she reluctantly let go and walked towards the garage to get her car out and ready for the drive home. Jan had seen it from the bed room window, she rushed down and walked out to Sophia. Ray watched them exchange a few words then hug, they then chatted about something but he could not hear what it was.

He walked into the shed and took out two large containers, they were used for carrying water but tonight they would be filled with petrol and he looked them over to make sure they were sound and not cracked or had holes in them. They were made from hard tough plastic and were battered but looked good and strong, a screw cap on top which meant he could get them to empty pretty quickly too.

When John came from the house just in his shorts he yawned and ambled over to Ray asking in a sleepy voice.

"Can I help in any way?"

"Yes, can you go and get these filled with petrol at the filling station please"

Ray dropped them both at his feet; he nodded and yawned again picking up the containers and walked back towards the house. Sophia got into her car and waved good bye, Jan had asked her to stay but she would not, she wanted to help Ray like she used to and that meant being in her home with her power and concentration.

Jan came up to Ray and folded her arms watching him check the oil on the dip stick from his car engine.

"You will promise me you will be safe of course" she said not looking at him but looking at the car engine as if she knew and understood what she was actually looking at.

"Well I will do my best of course" he said sliding the dip stick back into its hole.

"Want to borrow my gun; it came in handy last time you know"

"No, I will be ok but thank you anyway, thank you for everything you have done"

"Sophia has gone she wanted to be where she can help you the best apparently, but I think she just had to get away to fight her real feelings. She is a good woman, I was wrong about her when we first met but I think she is a good woman"

"That is very big of you to say Jan, not a lot of people admit their mistakes, you are a good woman too and I owe you a lot" he hugged her too and she responded likewise.

Bodie came trotting by and past them and then off into the garden, he sniffed the ground and then froze, Ray noticed and gently pushed Jan away without a word, he reached into his car, looking no more conspicuous then he should, he took the cross bow and loaded it out of sight in the boot, he glanced over at Bodie,, Jan backed up her heart beating faster she knew something was wrong. Bodie slowly walked and then stopped by a tree he sat and looked directly at Ray. It was all the sign he needed he spun round, aimed the bow into the upper branches of the tree and instantly found his target, a dweller peering down at them he gently squeezed the trigger letting the arrow fly fast silent and true. It hit the dweller in the chest throwing it back and out of the tree it awkwardly fell to the ground with a sickening thud and within a moment Bodie was onto it. Ray paid it no more attention and Jan gulped as she watched Bodie rip the thing to pieces.

"One less for me to deal with, looks like this place has been under surveillance all the time, so she will know I am here already" Ray said slamming the boot shut of his car.

"What shall we do then, will she come here?" Jan said looking round suddenly feeling scared.

"I want you safe Jan, so get yourself together and head home just be very careful and keep an eye out everywhere ok, I don't want anyone snatched and used as bait or anything"

"Fuck, you know how to calm a girl Ray you really do, just put me at ease I would" she looked round and then dashed into the house to get ready to leave.

He saw John come out and get into his car and take the containers with him he had no idea what had just happened, Ray walked over to where Bodie was stood over the dead and ripped open Body of the dweller, they both looked round and scanned the area, but both knew there was only one, just a look out, a watcher. But how long had they been watched and what had been reported back?

When Darius returned they disposed of what was left of the Dweller, everything Ray needed was now in the car. He would be setting off soon and leaving this place he hoped in peace. He had a good meal and said farewell to Jan, she left after lunch then Ray was about ready to go he wanted some alone time to run things over in his head he also wanted to go check the area while it was light enough just to familiarise himself once again, Darius thought it a bad idea, to risky but Ray felt it to be a good idea, he went with his instincts always and just knew he needed that time to familiarise himself with the place.

It was afternoon and would be getting dark soon, he was ready, he said good bye to Darius and John, they asked one more time to go with him but again he refused their offer. They watched him drive away, both hoping they would watch him drive back safely within twenty four hours.

It was back to normal, if his life could be called normal, Ray and Bodie out driving and ready to hunt down and destroy evil, they knew where it was they knew what it looked like, they just had to get the job done. He was going to check over the battle ground, the killing area, then lay low and rest until it was time for him to return and burn them out.

They parked up nearby and strolled along the path towards the woods, there was a couple walking hand in hand looking at each other and not really noticing Ray or Bodie as they strolled along, Ray searching for any abnormalities in the bushes and trees, he remembered where he found the entrance before and made sure it was still there, it was very well hidden but he could see it was a kind of trap door down into the tunnels no doubt, he took a mental note of where he was making a large distinctive elm tree has his point of reference, knowing the light would not be as good when he returned. Bodie marked a few spots himself knowing his scent would be a good marker for him later that night.

They walked through and took mental notes nothing happened and nothing seemed out of the ordinary but they both could sense the evil around it hung in the air like a stench. They walked through for a while and then back to the car, it had started to get dark and they drove away to rest up, he had seen what he wanted to see and was happy there was a large area near by the hatch he had discovered, a good fighting arena and killing ground.

He settled in his car and they both took a nap, the calm before the storm, he had been in this situation many times before and kept calm as he could, he just would take it has it came now and hoped he could get her before she had chance to do her black magic against them. He had no real idea what would happen and would fight on his wits and reaction and instincts. He would react to a situation and do whatever it took to win.

Darius was laid awake so was John, Darius had made Ray make sure his mobile phone was charged and made him promise to get in touch as soon as he could with any news. They were worried and knew as soon as light started to break the fight would be on and Ray would be in battle, Sophia had got home safe and was sat quiet, she was meditating and keeping herself calm. Jan had a drink in her hand and a bottle by her side she already had drank half of it she was waiting for dawn to break and then would wait for news of Ray, it was going to be a long night and she knew it, but no way would she sleep this night.

The darkness fell and the damp air came with it, a mild but humid night, Ray woke up and reached into his pocket and took out the small mobile phone, It was fully charged and he turned it on the screen lit up, illuminating the inside of the car a little, he then turned it off again and put it back into his pocket, Darius had insisted on him taking it and keeping in touch one way or another. He normally just doesn't bother with it but he promised and always liked to keep his promises. He closed his eyes and tried to relax, the night was going slow and he was just waiting for that twilight time just before the dawn breaks. He looked back and glanced at Bodie on the back seats he was stretched out and had his head on his front paws, he looked back at Ray, who turned and settled back into his seat he closed his eyes and tried to empty his mind and rest.

The woods were silent not even the animals were making a noise, it was unnaturally silent. But things started to move, things shifted in the darkness and the undergrowth. The dwellers were out and moving about, they were on guard and on watch. Angelique crawled awkwardly from a hold in the ground, she stood up and stretched out, and she lifted her nose and sniffed the air, turning her head to the side as she did.

"He has been here, I can smell the pig, he was here and he will return, where is the one we sent to watch them?" she asked but to no one in particular, two dwellers came and stood by her side. She scanned the area through the darkness and took deep breaths of air she was glad she could get out from the stinking tunnels now and breathe fresh air again. Her arms were hanging bent and deformed and they gave her pain she had adjusted to her situation but she didn't like it and was going to make that woman who shot her suffer when all this was over it had been a promise she had made herself. They walked round in the darkness for a while and the dwellers scurried for food. She just took deep breaths and mumbled to herself the dwellers left her be, and just went about their business. It would be several hours before they had done what they wanted.

CHAPTER NINE

Ray was awake and stretching outside of the car sometime later, Bodie jumped out also and stretched, it was time for them to go into battle. It was dark but the sun would be cutting through the blackness very soon and it would give them just enough light, he hoped. He took his knives and rested them in their secure places under his jacket and belt, the throwing knife down his boot. He went to the back of his car and opened the boot. Making sue the petrol containers were securely tied up so they could not fall over, the flares and the smoke bombs all there ready.

He knelt down and Bodie came to him and sat in front of him. Ray took the dog and hugged him; he stroked the back of his neck and rested his head on his. They stayed there for a moment and then he stood up and Bodie jumped into the back of the car, Ray closed the door and got in the front driver's seat and they were heading away moments later, in battle mode and ready to do whatever was needed to win this battle. He drove up to the woods and pulled his car into a clearing at the edge. He got out and looked round he could not sense anything but would be on the utmost guard and take no chances this night. He went to the back of the car and took out his rucksack he put the smoke bombs and flares in this and then lifted a petrol container out he put this on the ground then got the other one out too, he next took the two small butane gas bottles and put these on the ground next to them, he quietly closed his boot and flung the rucksack over his shoulder lifting a petrol container and a gas bottle he walked into the woods, Bodie sniffed the way by recognising the spots he had marked earlier that day, he took Ray straight to the hatchway they knew about. Ray quietly put the container and gas bottle down then swung the rucksack off his shoulder. He quickly went back to the car and brought the other two items back with him. He looked up and saw the darkness fading; he could start to make out shapes and things in the wood. Looking round he listened and Bodie did the same it was very silent, dampness all round. He knew of two entrances, so he took a smoke bomb and pulled the tab and threw this down the tunnel entrance shutting the hatch again when he did then he rushed the few dozen yards to the second one and did the same with a second smoke bomb. He could see the smoke rising even though it was still pretty dark. He noticed it escaping from a cluster of bushed to his left, he dashed over and pulled at them he could then see the hatch top covering another entrance. Suddenly it burst open spewing smoke up and out into the air, a dweller charged up and out disorganised and coughing Ray already had his knife in his hand and cut the throat of this beast, killing it before it knew what had happened. He turned and saw Bodie crouched listening, he had heard something and within seconds was on another dweller crawling from the hatchway. Dropping yet another smoke bomb down the hatch in front of him Ray then backed off and looked round. He was looking for the signs of other tunnel entrances or exits. Bodie took care of the dweller with ease and came next to Ray, the main it seemed there was only three hatchways here, he looked round and listened. Then he heard the voice, that hackle he would recognise anywhere, it was her, he dashed to the first hatch way, taking the petrol with him, he didn't bother to unscrew the cap he took his large knife plunged it into the top of the container and cut it round slicing the whole top off, he kicked the hatch open and backed off slightly as the smoke lifted, he then emptied the petrol down the hole. Suddenly the other two hatches were flung open and dwellers came out, two out of one and three out of the other, they screamed and dashed towards Ray. The battle commenced, Bodie pounced and took one out of mid air as it ran and jumped along, it was dead within seconds he had got the bite just right on the throat and ripped it out with ease. The others were charging towards Ray, Bodie was behind them catching them fast. Ray dodged to the left and slashed with his knife ha he did catching the attacking dweller across the mid section, spilling its blood onto the damp ground it squealed and rolled off to the side. Bodie already was there ripping into another and they fought fast and hard both of them disposing of the attacking creatures with brutal efficiency. Angelique could be heard from the hatchway shouting and screaming at these creatures. Ray pounded the last one into the ground knocking it senseless with his power and speed. He stood and looked round the dawn was breaking and the light was coming through. He noticed a dweller pulling at something from the main hatchway, it was helping Angelique out of the hold, and Ray dashed forward and kicked it back down the hole she looked at him with demonic eyes as she tumbled back down with it into the hole. Ray then went quickly to the flares on the ground he took one and ripped the bottom off and pulled the igniting cord, it flickered and then a bright blinding light burnt at one end he held it away from his face and then threw it down the hole where he had poured the petrol, it instantly woofed and engulfed in flames. Screams could be heard from the pit, Bodie dashed to the right, he had noticed movement from one of the other hatchways. Ray left him to deal with it. He edged over to the hole where the flames were coming up, dancing high. The damp grass and ground stopped it from catching fire. He heard the scream of Angelique and some other hideous noise of the dwellers as they burnt in there hole of flames, he could not get near and backed off has the intense heat raged flying from the hole.

Bodie was dragging a dweller from the other hatchway and Ray didn't even bother to watch he knew Bodie would handle the job easy. The third hatchway flew open and smoke bellowed out and also did the dwellers, one after another. Ray ran towards them and hit them while they were still confused and disorientated with the from the smoke and flames they had to deal with, He kicked and punched and sliced with his knives knocking them back and down stomping and crushing them under foot, one managed to pounce onto his back but he easily twisted and spun it off piercing its heart with his large knife has it fell and hit the ground. Bodie pounced and ripped and tore through whatever was in front of him, they both may have been out of action for a while but they were back now and better than ever. They fought with vengeance with courage and with a brutality that was unsurpassed. Anything that came for them was killed and destroyed they fought fast and with skill and efficiency. Suddenly there was a rumbling in the ground, a bright burst of flame shot up and a repulsive scream came from the depth of the burning hole. Ray spun and saw the burning figure of Angelique rise from the pit of flames, she was possessed by a demon she had summoned and it gave her power and strength, Ray dropped to one knee took out his throwing knife from his boot and threw it quickly it sliced through the air and hit her hard in the chest, she looked at it and laughed out at him. He was already running towards her both hands gripping the two remaining knives he had. The flames were dying down on her and she stood facing him, a vile contorted look on her face and death in her eyes she was holding her hands out towards him and screaming obscenities at him has he ran towards her. He dodged down as she swung and stuck his knife in her leg she dropped and spun round hitting out again, he moved fast and rolled away coming along the other side he stabbed again several times at her legs, then was out of reach straight away. Bodie was tearing the dwellers to pieces and keeping them off Ray while he dealt with Angelique, no more were coming from the hole and it was smoking black smoke from them, the flames seemed to of gone out now and just smoke bellowed up from the hatches. Ray rolled off and grabbed a butane bottle he turned the valve and the gas hissed out he threw this down the hole she had came from and then turned to just get out of the way of a vicious attack she raged against him with swiping clawed hands, he kicked out and caught her in the stomach, she was not as strong as she could of been and it was easier than he had expected. He sliced through her arm as she swung it at him, she screamed again when he punched her hard in the face splitting her nose and she bled wildly down her face, he grabbed her hair pulling her head down and back bringing his knife across her throat. She raged and tried to grab him but he had dropped her down onto his knee cracking her back painfully as he did so,

Her throat was gaping open and she was mumbling something, like a chant she closed her eyes and went limp. He managed to throw her to the ground and kick her over she looked up at him and a smile came across her face, she then started to laugh, he kicked her again and rolled her to the hole and pushed her down it. He could hear her laughing has she fell back down into the smoked filled and gas infected hole. He lifted a dead dweller and threw this down the hole too and then backed away, he saw that Bodie was coming by his side and then motioned him away. He ran over and picked up the dead dwellers and threw them down the hatchways until they were all gone he was breathing heavy and opened the second butane gas bottle throwing this down the hatch he backed off looking round he made a quick scan of the area, the laugh of Angelique could be heard gargling through her sliced throat, Ray took a flare, he ripped the bottom off and pulled the small cord he threw this has it ignited down the hatchway, the gas ignited and the blast was strong, it shook the ground and the surrounding trees shuddered, the underground tunnels started to collapse, flames shot up from each hatch way and the tunnels caving in on themselves, rumbling deep in the earth. Then there was silence once again, the ground was still. the smoke bellowed and the flash of the ignited gas was gone, the holes were caved in and filled with earth and soil, and it was quiet. They both slowly walked to the hatchway Ray stamped out some burning leaves and grass as he did, he looked in and saw it was solid with soil and the walls had crumbled in on themselves, he wasted no time and began to clear the area as much as he could, pulled branches and bushes and placed them over the hatchways, it was not perfect but it was better than nothing he picked up the last petrol container and the rucksack and they both hurried back to the car. Moving fast they made good pace and distance the light was stronger and the darkness going quickly. Reaching his car they both stood motionless for a moment, it was a feeling they both had simultaneously. They looked at each other and then Bodie walked forward, he heard it first, then Ray heard it too, a faint howl, If he allowed it, his heart would of been gripped with fear, they both looked up to the hillside and then saw the sight they hoped they would never see again, the beast was stood snorting and then sniffing the air, silhouetted on the hill side it then suddenly started to charge down towards them, he realised what Angelique was laughing at now when she was just about to die, she had summoned back the beast with her last breath. The same beast that had almost killed them both, but there was no Jan with her automatic to fill its head full of lead this time, they were alone and it was charging down towards them fast. Ray looked round desperate to find something, all he had was the petrol container, he quickly took his knife and stabbed the top slicing the top off so he could get it all out faster.

"Distract it Bodie, distraction lad" he said to his dog while he looked back up at the large bulk of the ferociousness bearing down on them. he took the last flare and tucked it in his belt, this was going to be hard and his only chance, he knew he was no match for it one on one, he had already tried that and was not going to try it again. He looked in the rucksack, one smoke bomb left. Bodie moved forward bravely and the hair rose on his spine he growled and bared his teeth. Ray stood next to him and they both looked at this fearless killing machine charging towards them, Ray took the smoke bomb in his hand and his large knife in his other, they had nowhere to run and didn't want to take it out in to where they could be seen. It was here and now. It was going to be at this spot that their fate was decided and the fight ended one way or another. Ray looked round and got his bearings he moved to the left of Bodie who walked to the right; his job was to distract however he could and he would do his utmost to protect his master even if it meant giving his life.

The howl was loud and blood curdling the savage, ferocity and power of this thing was tremendous. It was almost there it leaped over a fence from the neighbouring field and charged across the open ground towards them. Ray took the smoke bomb and armed it then threw it in the path of this monster, it blew up and sent clouds of thick black smoke into the air, as soon as it blew Ray dashed to the left and Bodie to the right. The beast charged through the smoke but had to stop in its tracks and turn, they were gone. Bodie then ran across its path, it turned its head quickly and snarled at him Ray dashed across in the opposite direction it turned again and went for where Ray was. Ray quickly did a forward roll and headed for the smoke to cover him; the beast lashed out but missed him. No sooner had Ray passed it Bodie dashed in and bite and tore at the leg of the beast then was gone. Just distracting it enough for it to take its eyes off where Ray had gone, it roared out in frustration and leaped through the smoke that was not dispersing, as it landed back on the ground Ray took his chance and leaped up at the same time he landed on the back on the thing and instantly used his knife to stab at its eyes. He was lucky and hit one, blinding it but before he could get the other eye he was spun off violently to the ground. Bodie again ran in and attacked giving Ray a few moments to get to his feet, and then both Ray and Bodie zigzagged in front of this half blinded beast it turned one way then the other, blood pouring from its left blinded eye. Ray wanted to try and get the second eye but it was being too aggressive and protective he had no chance of getting near he knew one savage blow from this powerful thing could end him and he had been there before and didn't want to return. He ran towards the petrol and lifted the container up, he nodded to Bodie who barked and snarled and snapped at the legs of the beast, making it turn momentarily which was all Ray needed he dashed forward and threw the contents all over the face and body of the beast drenching it in the petrol, then he rolled away and was on his feet crisscrossing with Bodie in front of the beast again, it turned and swung out at them but missed. Ray waved Bodie away and the dog ran and crouched a few yards away. Ray took the flare from his belt pulled the cord the bright burning fire at the end lit up and he had to hold it away from his self he had one chance and knew it, he ran towards the half blinded beast and rammed the flare deep into its fur igniting it instantly then he dashed off away as the flames caught and engulfed the screaming beast it lifted onto its hind legs and howled out in pain and torment. Bodie barked at it, more in excitement than anything the inferno caught well and the fur was burnt off and the beast fell to the ground, disorientated, and then quickly turned its head to look at Ray opening its one good eye it stared at him the flames burning its flesh. Running to his car he opened the boot and reached in he took his cross bow, he quickly pulled the draw string and got the bow ready. Putting the arrow in the grove he came round and stood staring at this thing that was intent on killing him, with nerves of steel he looked through the sights of the bow and aimed for the remaining eye this was going to be the most important shot of his life, he had only one chance and he knew it all too well. He squeezed the trigger as the beast was charging towards him, on fire the fur burning up fiercely, causing it to be screaming and howling, standing steady he holds his ground, Bodie is ready to leap just in case it goes wrong, Ray lets the arrow fly it hits bulls eye and blinds the burning beast piercing through its brain and sticks out the other side of its skull about six inches Ray dashes to the side and out of the way the bulk of the beast lunged forward, blinded, on fire and shaking its head, reaching up to its face and eyes with its large powerful hands. Ray reloaded his bow he knelt down on one knee and took aim again this time the arrow went through the throat ripping the jugular and causing the beast to fall back and down, the flames burning it up tearing at its own flesh in a frenzy of panic and anger and demented torture of pain it tried to pull the arrows out, but it was blinded and on fire. Ray put the bow back and reached far into the boot to get his axe, this was going to end now and this was going to be bloody. The beast rolled to its side and tried to get to its feet. Ray was already there and brought the axe down hard across the back of its neck, cutting deep it screamed out and reached up but it was too slow and blinded Ray had already moved swinging the axe down again he severed its foot, rolling in agonising pain it lashed out blindly but once again Ray was gone and moved round he brought the axe down once again and split the head in two, spilling brains and matter all over the ground and the beast dropped lifeless, he took no chances and continued with several more blows of the axe to sever the head also. There was a change in the flames and they turned black he stood back the axe in his hand ready, Bodie came by his side they watched as the fire intensified and burnt up the body of the beast. It seemed to strip it then down to bone and the fire raged up and it was gone, vaporized into the air. Just leaving a scorched mark where it had been. Wasting no time Ray packed the things back into the boot of the car and was gone. He drove quickly and headed away.

While he did he took the mobile phone from his pocket and quickly sent Darius a text.

"She is dead; I am heading away thanks for everything"

He threw the phone down and took a deep breath, Bodie was on the back seat resting and they both felt pretty good a great weight had been lifted and the job was done. They had conquered what they set out to do and survived. It had been a strange time and a very testing time, but at least they had survived and also he had made a new friend and ally.

Some hours later he pulled up outside the house, the door opened and Sophia stood there and smiled at him. He got out of his car and stretched and so did Bodie. They both stood and looked at her. Her smile broadened.

"Put the kettle on love, have you any biscuits?" he asked has he and Bodie walked in.

The End

To be continued with   Hunters in Darkness

L - #0188 - 071019 - C0 - 210/148/7 - PB - DID2639733